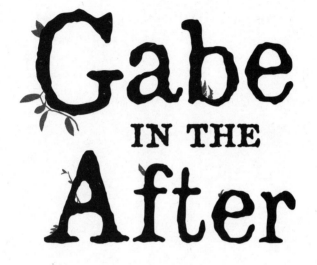

Gabe
IN THE
After

AMULET BOOKS • NEW YORK

Gabe

IN THE

After

SHANNON
DOLESKI

Cataloging-in-Publication Data has been applied for and may be obtained from the Library of Congress.

ISBN 978-1-4197-5438-8

Text © 2022 Shannon Doleski
Illustrations © 2022 Minnie Phan
Book design by Jade Rector

Printed and bound in U.S.A.
10 9 8 7 6 5 4 3 2 1

Amulet Books are available at special discounts when purchased in quantity for premiums and promotions as well as fundraising or educational use. Special editions can also be created to specification. For details, contact specialsales@abramsbooks.com or the address below.

Amulet Books® is a registered trademark of Harry N. Abrams, Inc.

ABRAMS The Art of Books
195 Broadway, New York, NY 10007
abramsbooks.com

To Gilbert Blythe and Anne Shirley

It was Gabe's day to check for survivors.

The boy hung the binoculars the scouts used around his neck and headed for the shore. He whistled, and his shoes crunched on the rocks. His dog, a German short-haired pointer named Mud, danced next to him.

The wind was stronger down by the water, and salt sprayed his face lightly. He stopped, checked the boat for damage, and lifted the binoculars to his face again.

Gabe scanned the opposite shore. Before the world ended, the town across the water had been a small hub with a lighthouse and marina. The ferry would cross three times a day. Eight. Noon. And six. But now that was over. The lighthouse didn't warn anyone of danger from the rocky coast.

It was still there, the lighthouse, but it was broken. A storm had damaged the glass, and there had been no one to repair it.

A pale gray bird stretched its wings and flew over the water. When no other movement disrupted the scene, Gabe let the binoculars rest against his chest. He busied himself with the boat, checked again for any blemishes in the wood like Peter had showed him, and picked up the oars.

He liked scout day. He liked being alone for a little bit. And it was something different from the usual chores of the island. Instead of mucking out stalls or making dinner for everyone, he was in charge of finding out if anyone had survived. He liked that responsibility and potential.

And sure, no one had ever been at the red post during the two years he'd been checking, but still, he had a fresh burst of hope that maybe, just maybe, this would be the day that someone was waiting at the stump of wood with the sign that said: ARE YOU A SURVIVOR IN NEED OF HELP? WAIT HERE, AND SOMEONE WILL COLLECT YOU AT NOON. For all they knew, whole sections of the world could have survived.

He wanted to be the one to find the survivor. It was the closest thing to scoring a winning shot in a game, and he missed that feeling. Sylvia would be proud. The other kids would think he was important. He didn't *want* to want to be the one, but he hoped that he was.

Gabe dragged the boat to the water. He was careful not to let his boots get wet, though they were waterproof. The water was cold. Cold Atlantic blue. Once, he had been to Key West in Florida, and the water was not cold. It was the same ocean, but it wasn't cold. It didn't seem fair.

He wondered if there were survivors in Key West. Maybe there was a spot at the southern tip of Florida full of kids in pastel-colored houses who had somehow survived, like the twenty of them had on his island.

But it was doubtful. *Wouldn't they have heard from someone by now?*

Gabe sat in the middle of the rowboat. There were three life preservers. Just in case. He pushed the oar into the small pebbles of the shore. He leaned all his weight on it, and the boat slid into the water.

He sang a song as he rowed, one that Malachi had been humming all week. A song that had been popular when they were little. Malachi sang it as a joke, and then the rest of them had joined in. Sylvia let them play it on

Saturday, the day they were allowed to use the solar panels for fun. The song was stuck in Gabe's head. Maybe for eternity. He sang it over and over. Sang it low and high, changing his voice, and laughed. He was glad no one could hear him.

He remembered a birthday party where the song had blared over and over again. They'd eaten chocolate cake, and his sister, Caroline, had gotten dark frosting all over her teeth and they had laughed so hard, he almost peed his pants. He missed her and chocolate cake.

Gabe's throat felt full. He wrinkled his nose so he wouldn't cry and called out, "Mud, do you see any fish?" to distract himself. His dog stood at the front of the boat, and her brown ears tipped side to side as she gazed into the water.

He cleared his throat. Maybe there would be a survivor.

When the boat hit the opposite shore, he turned around and looked back. There were two islands in the small bay. They called them the big and the small island, though they had other, official names. Only the small island was visible from the mainland. It was two miles long and a mile wide. From here, it didn't look inhabited. Sylvia said it kept them safe. From what, they didn't know, but it made sense that the end of the world would make people desperate.

He pulled up the boat until it rested against the big riprap under the lighthouse. He shouted, for fun. "Hello!" And the waves answered back behind him. He hooked the sheathed knife they used to gut fish around his shoulder.

Gabe held the binocular straps against him as he hopped up onto a piece of the dock. It ended jagged and abrupt over the water. Probably from the same storm that had knocked out the windows high above. Once, he and Malachi had inspected the lighthouse. They had scavenged what they could. A small painting of the island that was now in Sylvia's room. A mirror for the downstairs bathroom after Tim had broken their own. A cat they'd tried to capture, but she'd refused.

He saw her now, bright orange like the carrots they grew in the side garden, licking her paw. She looked at Gabe and rolled onto her back as if she wanted to be petted. But Gabe knew, because he had tried before, that she would not allow it.

"Hey, Carrots," he said.

The cat leaped up and darted into the weeds alongside the building. Mud trotted after her and disappeared into the green. Gabe didn't like when Mud went too far out of his sight. It made his heart race.

"Mud, I'm going to the post." It was a short walk down a lush, overgrown sandy path, plants stretching out as far as they could. He looked to his left and right occasionally and peered through his lenses. Nothing besides the Maine wilderness.

At the post, he stopped and whistled for his dog. Gabe placed his palm on top of the rough wood, where it wasn't painted red. He sighed and looked at his wrist. He would wait for one hour. That's what they always did. Every day for almost two years.

Gabe sat on the path and unsheathed the knife. He traced a circle in the sandy gravel. And another around that. And another. He stood up and brushed them all away with his foot. He sighed again. He wished he had a phone to distract himself. This was an errand, and before, when his mom had run errands, he would be on his phone. Stupid videos and talking to his friends. Sometimes his sister would make him team up online in role-playing games where they robbed banks, and he pretended it was annoying. It wasn't.

He sighed a third time. That's why he needed a phone. So he didn't have to think about his sister.

"Is anyone out there?" he yelled at the trees, so loudly that his throat immediately ached.

And then he heard something.

A cry from the woods.

2

"Mud?"

Gabe ran toward the sound, his knife out and ready. He sprinted into the dark of the woods, breathing hard, past the pine trees that rose above the coast.

Was it his dog? Was it a human? Had he imagined it? He didn't know.

"Muddy!" he yelled again. He could hear the panic in his voice.

Sylvia and Peter hadn't really told him what to do if he found a survivor. *Fight them if they were dangerous? Bring them back to the island?* No one had told him. It was always how to look for survivors, not what to do if there were any.

He burst through the trees. In the clearing, surrounded by green ferns, was a girl with a flame of hair.

Gabe stopped. He had been hoping for this moment for days. Weeks. Months. Years.

A survivor.

But also, a sharp prick of fear ran through him. *What if she was dangerous?*

Gabe didn't know what to do. He kept his knife ready. He was nervous. He wasn't often nervous. And when he was, he was able to fake confidence well.

"Who are you?" he asked. She looked about his age. Maybe thirteen or fourteen. She had pale skin and seemed around his height. Looped around her shoulder was a duffel bag.

He couldn't remember the last time he'd met someone new. He scowled and tried to recall a new classmate, a new friend. But his mind couldn't pull the memory.

When he was in third grade, the Andrews family had been new. But that was so long ago. There had to have been other introductions. It bothered him when he couldn't remember things that had happened before. It felt like it was slipping away from him. Which was annoying, because how could this new world be anywhere as good as the old one?

But here was a new meeting, a new person. However it went, he wanted to remember it.

The knife ready, he didn't move, and neither did the girl.

Her mouth was open, gaping. She had bright freckles covering her face and her wrists and hands. No one on the island had freckles. He frowned. *Why did he think of that?*

The girl still hadn't answered. Gabe wondered if she spoke a different language and tried Spanish. French. "Como te llamas? Comment t'appelles-tu?" He was a little impressed with himself that he could remember that in a time like this.

But her mouth just stayed open. She clutched her heart.

A crash came from the bushes, and Gabe gripped the knife handle tight and braced his knees.

Out spilled a brown dog. Mud ran toward the stranger and wiggled her butt. The girl dropped down and cradled the furry face in her hands. Her hair poured over the dog so that all Gabe saw was red.

Gabe softened a bit. He lowered his knife. But he did not sheathe it. She seemed like she wouldn't . . . well, she wouldn't stab him with some weapon hidden on her.

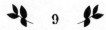

The boy pursed his mouth. He was still wary. "I live over there," he said. "On the island." He pointed behind him. He knew the trees covered the view of the water, but it was something. The air smelled like salt. "Where do you live?" And because that felt rude, he added, "What's your name?"

"I always thought, if I saw another person—which I truly wasn't expecting, were you? How delightful! Do you meet many people now? If you have, I would guess it has not been congenial, based on the knife—I would tell them Cecilia. I thought it over and decided that it is my very favorite name in the whole world. Would you call me Cecilia?" Her voice was very bright.

It was a strange thing to say, but he was about to tell her "Okay," since little Bear had named himself Bear, when she interrupted him. "But that isn't my real name. My real name was a gift from my parents, and don't I miss them more than anything? So if I want to honor their memory"—she bowed her head against Mud's—"I should accept their gift. My name is Relle Douglas."

Relle. He had never heard that name before. "I'm Gabe Sweeney," he said.

She looked up. The girl had huge eyes. They were green. "That's a nice name." She stood. "I read once, that if you gave your real name, your true name, the other person could steal your power. That was in a story. It was a lovely story with dragons and puffs of smoke. I loved that description. It was so palpable, like I could touch it. Do you know the story?"

Her voice was very earnest. It made him uncomfortable. Like she was sharing way too much and too quickly. Like he could hear every feeling in every letter she said.

Gabe cleared his throat. "I don't."

"I spent three months in a library. It was deliciously quiet. I wasn't so lonely with all those stories around me. Each book was an adventure, and I was the heroine. When the roof started to cave in from a leak, I had to leave. I was dreadfully sad when that happened."

He knew she was sad. He could feel it.

Gabe took a step back. She was very strange. A strange girl in the woods. And if he believed in stories, in fairy tales, like this girl probably did, he would have thought she wasn't real. "Are you real?" he asked, more to himself than to her.

Maybe he had a fever like they'd all gotten last fall. Maybe he had eaten a bad fruit. Once that had happened to Delia, Malachi's sister. Or maybe he was dreaming. Those were the only plausible explanations.

"Am *I* real?" Relle asked. "Are *you*? I do have a habit of inventing people." The girl took two fingers and pinched herself on the forearm. She squeaked.

Gabe imitated her, though not with the same enthusiasm, and felt the sharp pain of being awake and alive.

With the confirmation that they were real, Relle launched into a dozen questions. Hundreds of questions. One after another. All he could do was wait until she stopped for air.

"I live on the island, yeah, with some others from the big island," he started. "There are twenty of us. Eighteen kids and two adults. We all came here the summer the world ended."

"The summer the world ended," she repeated. Her eyes shone. "How romantically tragic sounding, Gabe. You're right, it did end. Or what we knew ended. After all, we are here, the trees are flourishing, these glorious ferns exist."

She was right. He hadn't really noticed, but now he saw that the ferns were nice. And so was the sun that blinked above the pines. The combination made his whole chest warm and happy. Gabe's dad had always been good at changing his son's mind with one sentence. And apparently so was this girl.

"Is that what you call it? The end of the world?" she asked.

Gabe nodded and shrugged. That's what they all called it. He didn't know who started it, but for some reason he wanted Relle to believe it was him—if she liked it. He didn't want to lie, though.

"What do you call it?" he asked.

The new girl frowned. She tipped her head. Gabe noticed she had a pretty chin. And then *he* frowned because he had never had that specific thought before, that someone had a pretty chin. He knew Violet and Chloe were pretty. Had been pretty before and after the end of the world, but he hadn't studied their faces quite so intently before.

He didn't know what that meant exactly.

"I guess I call it the After," she answered, "which isn't half as dramatic as yours and not nearly as gut-wrenching, so I will call it the summer the world ended as well." She waved her arm in the air like she was announcing a movie title.

Gabe was proud. Really proud. He puffed right up, his shoulders back. He wanted her approval. He also wanted to ask her a million questions himself. *Where are you from? How did you get here? Are there others? Who else?* He felt like if

he didn't ask the questions immediately and absorb the information, he would run out of time.

And he knew that was stupid, because they had too much time for talking on the island, so maybe he should relax, slow it down. Even though he was buzzing like when his lacrosse team had won their tournament when he was ten.

It was hard to control.

He thought practically. If she came back with him to the little island, he could ask her as many questions as he wanted. Sylvia would expect him soon. It took, depending on the tide, around thirty to forty minutes to make it across the channel. And even though he'd have to share the new girl with the others once they arrived—the thought both annoyed him and made him feel guilty—he'd have those minutes in the boat to ask Relle questions and listen to her strange answers.

"Do you want to come to our island?" he asked.

3

Gabe walked ahead and Relle followed behind him. Mud wove in and out between the kids and the fields and the trees. Maine had always been wild, but without people to mow and prune and trim, it was a spring jungle. Relle burst out with, "Stop pouting, Roy!" and then, "And watch the ferns!"

Gabe stopped and turned. Was there another survivor? "Is there someone else with you?" he asked.

Relle blushed. "Roy is . . ." She shifted her feet. Green things stuck out of her hair, maybe ferns. Gabe couldn't tell whether she'd put them there on purpose. "Roy is a romantic figure of my own creation. He bloomed from my head. He is a combination of a boy from my math class, a girl singer, and a character from a book. He's very dashing but temperamental."

Gabe bit the inside of his lip. He didn't want her to think he was laughing at her, because he didn't think he was. It was more that he couldn't help the smile from slamming into him.

"How do you get across the water?" she asked. Her face was as red as her hair.

Gabe assumed she was changing the subject, so he played along. "We have a boat, a rowboat. Since we don't use gas." There was no gas on the island, and Peter said it wouldn't last long anyway. The shelf life for it was short, a few years. And Mud's nails slipped on the kayak when he took that, so the rowboat it was.

They walked toward the red post. Relle stopped next to it. It reached her shoulder.

"Did you make this?" she asked.

"Sylvia," he said. "She's kind of our leader."

"Will you tell me about her? About all of the others too. Are you a family?" Relle scurried close to him, and he froze. He didn't usually freeze. *What was wrong with him?*

"Some of us, yes," he said. A burning ached in his throat. Wynnie had their sister. Malachi had his. All four

Andrews kids had made it to the little island. He did not mention how unfair it was that they still had family left. How envious he was. How it was hard to see them together sometimes.

"My family did not make it," Relle said. "I would very much like to belong to people again. I feel this aching part of me yearning for a family. It's what kept me walking."

A great big silence rested between them, and Gabe was anxious to fill it. But he couldn't speak.

"I suppose families need to be found sometimes," Relle said. "Like a missing pen."

Gabe felt a rush of joy.

He pointed at the lighthouse and told her about it. The trees around it were already blossoming. They walked down to the shore, and he showed her where he had stored the boat. She helped him drag it to the edge of the water.

Gabe wiped his hands on his pants, tan ones that someone had brought back from one of the summer shops on the big island. Some of them went once or twice a month to get supplies. But Gabe never did. He couldn't. It was a ghost town, and he knew all the ghosts. He didn't know how the others could go back and go shopping.

Relle needed some new clothes, he noticed. Hers were too small. Her striped yellow shirt sleeves were too short, and between her boots and jeans a patch of pale skin showed. Gabe's mom would take him shopping in Portland whenever he had a growth spurt. They couldn't just drive down 95 when that happened now, though.

"Just in case." He handed Relle a life preserver. "Can you swim?"

"I can," she said. "I'm a good swimmer. I used to race on a team in the summers in Boston. I am very competitive and fast. Relays are my favorite, though we won't be racing in any relays today."

Gabe was also very competitive. Well, he had been. He hadn't felt very competitive lately. He wondered if she was faster than him and Malachi. In a month or so, when Sylvia declared it warm enough for the beach, they could race. Today was not warm enough. The foam was white as it hit the gray pebbles.

"How can I be helpful?" she asked. "I can row. We can take turns. Or we can each have an oar."

"Okay," Gabe said. He showed her where to sit, and she did. He sat across from her, and Mud took her spot at the head of the boat, front paws on the prow. "We can take turns."

Gabe tried not to stare—at the stranger who didn't feel much like a stranger—when it was his turn to rest. The idea that he was returning to the island with a survivor was . . . well, he didn't know what it was. It was unbelievable almost. But here she was.

He was used to rowing, but Relle looked like she was a beginner. She was trying, though. Her eyebrows were pushed together, and she was talking, but huffing as she did. And her arms were skinny and awkward with the oars. Gabe didn't mind if it took them longer. He enjoyed having a new person to talk to.

"Tell me about them all," she said. "So I know what to expect. Are they kind? Is there bread?"

Gabe smiled. He liked her. He was having to hold back smiles so she didn't think he was laughing at her. But everything she said was weird and made this uncomfortable and happy feeling in his chest.

She wiped her hair from her forehead with the back of her hand and kept rowing. She still had plants in her hair, stuck in the red. Christmas colors. Gabe wondered what he would have thought about her Before. If they had shared a class or something.

He didn't think they would have been friends. Well, maybe they would have. They wouldn't have been enemies at least. Gabe didn't have enemies.

Yes, he decided. They would have been friends. Before, he had been friends with a boy named Steven, who was a little like Relle. Different and in his own world.

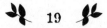

Gabe sighed. Steven did not live on the little island.

"Well, there's Sylvia," he told her. "She's pretty organized and serious. She owned a café on the big island, and now she's kind of like our teacher or something. I don't know." One of the science teachers at the high school had recommended sending everyone without symptoms to the little island. Sylvia had been the only adult without the rash on her cheeks. She had piloted the boat. At first, they thought staying in the big house would be temporary. Gabe had packed a bag with only five outfits.

He cleared his throat. "Peter. He's the other adult. He's quiet. He used to be the caretaker of the house, so he still does that. He stays out in the barn a lot. He's old and has some heart problems."

Gabe looked behind him. They were almost to the island. "Do you want to . . . do you have a mirror and want to clean up before we meet everyone? I don't . . . you have . . ." He pointed to his own hair.

Relle scowled. "I have a mirror, Gabe." She passed the oars to him, her face red again. He bit his lip. Why did everything she say make his cheeks hurt? It was disconcerting.

And she had said his name. He thought about what she'd said, that knowing someone's true name gave you power. *Did she have power over him? Was she even real?* He'd find out soon when they reached the others. He hoped he hadn't made her up. What a weird daydream, if he had.

No, he was certain his brain hadn't made her up. Relle was picking pine boughs out of her hair. He would not have made that up.

"Tell me about the kids," she said. She stuck her chin out.

"Malachi is my best friend. He's funny. We played lacrosse together. And Wynnie. Wynnie's pronouns are they/them. You'll like them. Everyone likes Wynnie because they're nice and friendly."

He told her about little Bear, the youngest, and his sister, Delphine, who had been his neighbors on Sea Lane. He told her about Lucas, who was great at music, and Eric, who was seventeen and not especially nice. He told her about the girls, Violet and Chloe.

"Your family?" she asked.

His expression must have given away his thoughts.

She put her hand to her chest and leaned forward, so that she was looking right into his heart, it felt like.

He shook his head. And then, because she was too earnest, too sincere, he scooted back on the slim bench under him until he was almost falling off.

"Oh, Gabe," she said with so much air, "I am so sorry. I know what it's like to be an orphan. At first, I talked to my mom and dad when I started walking, but then I realized that was too hard and too sad. So I stopped in the woods and shared the most beautiful memories I could think of about both of them, and then I met Roy. Roy hurts my heart a little less." She nodded. "I'll go back home someday for a proper farewell."

Gabe did not share about his parents or sister. He thought it was a bit silly that Relle had made up a person instead of remembering real people, who loved you and cared about you, even when you were annoying or had a pimple or bad breath. But he kept that to himself.

When they reached the shore, Gabe hopped out first, then offered a hand to Relle. She took it and stepped out of the boat, her other arm parallel to the rocky coast.

He didn't want to let her hand drop.

And he didn't want to not want to drop it.

He and Violet had kissed behind the barn. After dinner a week ago. And after the thrill of it wore off, he felt terrible, because she liked him much more than he liked her. Now it seemed an even bigger mistake somehow.

He didn't know why. He ran his hand over his hair. "Are you ready?" he asked.

"To meet my family?" she asked. She clutched her duffel bag in her hands. "I'm not sure anyone is ever ready to meet a new family. But I expect I am as ready as I ever will be. I hope they love me."

Gabe didn't know what to think. On the one hand, how could she replace her family like that? With people she didn't know. The island, the twenty survivors, could be full of terrible humans as far as she knew, and she was just . . . well, he didn't understand it. Not at all.

But one tiny sliver of him, the smallest bit, was in awe.

She didn't talk like the world had ended. She talked like it was just beginning.

4

Gabe pulled the boat all the way up to the grasses that swayed in the wind. Relle turned and waved goodbye to the mainland.

They walked down a green path, and Gabe explained the history of the island. How it used to be owned by a rich family, the Glovers, who'd spent summers there. And when the last Glover died, it was donated to the state as a historical site, and tourists visited in the summer. They'd take the ferry for the day, picnic on the lawn, tour the house, and pretend they were millionaires. Gabe had been here a bunch of times, Before. His family visited the mansion for kite-flying festivals.

At first, when Gabe and the other kids were brought here, they waited and waited to go home. They filled their time playing basketball and roaming the mansion. They camped out in one of the living rooms. Then they stopped hearing from their families. They lost phone service. After a week went by, Peter took a boat across the channel. Gabe didn't know what he had found, but he heard rumors from the other kids. No survivors. No way to contact the outside world. Nothing.

Sylvia decided they wouldn't wait anymore. They would get ready for the Maine winter. They would survive. Now they had school and chores. Scheduled free time in the evenings. On Saturdays, they watched movies on a projector in the living room or played video games. Sundays, the kids who wanted to pray or have services did, but no one was required to.

Gabe told Relle all this as the green path turned into a dirt road. He did not mention how even though they did those things, the chores and school and routines, he still felt like he was waiting. Like he was in a waiting room and the doctor was running late. Like he wasn't sure the doctor was ever going to call him in to the appointment. Instead, he sighed.

On each side of the road, great trees grew, white flowers blooming along their branches. Relle stopped. "Oh, Gabe," she said. "Oh, Gabe, what is this?"

The way she said his name was too much. He had to clear his throat. *Get it together, Sweeney*, he told himself. It was so stupid. He barely knew her. *Answer her question!* "We call it the Avenue. That's what it said in the house. There's a map on the wall."

"You know, if I hadn't been wandering in the woods yelling at Roy exactly when I was, I wouldn't be here on your island now. On this beautiful path to a family." Relle turned to him. "I'm so glad we found each other, Gabe Sweeney. The very stars made our meeting happen. It was fate that made us meet, don't you think?"

It was impossible to answer. Both because he couldn't talk for some unknown reason and also because Gabe was very practical. He didn't believe in fate. So he did the only thing he could. He nodded.

"I could stay here for the rest of my life," she said. "Maybe I'll bring a blanket and spread it out and sleep under the stars. Only I'm sure I wouldn't be able to sleep, it's that pretty."

Gabe was positive he needed the others to break this weird spell. "It's not much farther to the house."

"This is why it took me two years to walk. I get very

distracted and my mind wanders. I wonder if I did see other people in my travels, but I was too far into a daydream to notice. Once I thought two men had been following me, but it was my imagination." She laughed. "Yes, let's meet the others."

And that's when they were spotted. First, the two youngest, Bear and Delphine, and then the others. The entire island was running toward them. Mud zigzagged, spun, and barked. Gabe felt a rush of excitement.

"Gabe!" Lucas shouted. He was tall with pale skin and big blue eyes. "What? Where did . . . ? How?"

The whole group started talking at the same time, their eyes on the new girl.

"She was in the woods," Gabe said. He wanted to say he found her, but that would sound like he was bragging.

"I'm Relle Douglas," she said. "Pleased to meet you."

The kids stopped talking for a beat, because she had spoken. And then they shouted excitedly all at once. An explosion of noise and movement and frenzy.

Gabe headed toward the house, and the rest of them swirled around him and Relle like a school of fish. They passed the orchard and the large garden that Peter had made with the heirloom seeds from the hardware store on the big island.

The group didn't stop to pet the goats like they usually did. They moved on to the driveway, the big half-circle of gravel, and up the stairs to the brick mansion where they lived now. Gabe had been sharing the navy-blue bedroom with Malachi and Lucas for almost two years, but he didn't think of it as home. His real bedroom was across the channel.

"What a beautiful house," Relle said.

The kids stopped and stared at her again.

It *was* a beautiful house, and now that they were totally off-grid, it was basically its own power plant. Solar panels covered the roof and powered their electricity. Once, when the grid first went down, the power went out for three days. Peter realized they had nowhere to store the energy the panels produced on sunny days, so he attached a dozen batteries used in trolling motors. When it was cloudy, the house used the energy stored in the batteries. A few months later, when a big winter storm hit the island and the sun didn't shine for a week, they were able to stay safe and warm.

"We're so happy to have you here," Wynnie said. "I'm Wynnie." Wynnie was tall with broad shoulders, a long cloud of black hair, and a tan even in the Maine winter. They wore khakis and a button-down shirt every day, except when they played basketball, which they were very

good at. Gabe liked being on their team because they set up screens well.

"I am happy to be here too, Wynnie," Relle said. "I think we'll be good friends." She latched onto Wynnie, and Gabe felt a pang of jealousy. He did not think the group was breaking the spell. In fact, he knew they were under it as well.

As they reached the front door, it opened. Sylvia stood in the doorway, wiping her hands on a dish towel. She was tall and slim with deep brown skin. "What is this fuss about?" she asked. "Who is this?" She looked from Relle to Gabe and back again.

"I am Relle Douglas from Boston, well, Lowell, Massachusetts. Have you been? I wandered up the coast of Maine, living on peanut butter mostly." She wrinkled her nose. "If I never see another jar of peanut butter, I will consider it a success. Yes, it was only me and my peanut butter, and Roy, of course."

"Roy?" Sylvia asked.

Gabe squirmed. *Was Relle going to tell them all about her imaginary friend?* "She was in the woods, Sylvia," he explained.

"Roy is my closest companion," Relle answered. "But he is not a real person, so he will not require shelter or sustenance in the traditional sense."

A pair of giggles escaped Bear and Delphine. When

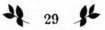

29

they were babies, they had moved from Korea to the house next to Gabe's. Now they were six.

"We haven't seen a survivor," Violet said. "A real survivor here! On the island! And all because of Gabe."

Violet gazed up at him, and Gabe was . . . well, he wanted to escape the stare, even if it was a pretty one with long eyelashes and a full mouth. When they were little, Violet had gotten in trouble for running around the playground kissing the boys. Gabe realized the barn kiss was probably not their first kiss, but maybe their second or third or fourth. Not that elementary school kisses counted.

"Hmm, we haven't seen a survivor," Sylvia said. She regarded Relle with a look of hesitation. "I thought that post was a good idea, to help one another, but maybe it's dangerous."

Relle turned bright red. Her eyes filled with tears. And for the second time that day, Gabe did not know what to do.

"You don't want me?" Relle whispered.

Sylvia looked Relle over. Gabe wanted to shout, *Let her stay! Please, Sylvia!*

"Now, now, I didn't say that," Sylvia said. "You're a child. I'm just thinking out loud about other survivors. I don't know if we ever expected to find another person. It's shocking to us all."

Violet was crying now, along with Relle, their hands locked together. "She can stay, right, Sylvia?" Violet asked.

"Of course she may stay," Sylvia said. She turned and walked into the house, and the island followed. "The rest of us have eaten, but let me get you two lunch. I assume you're hungry. Come, Relle. You can tell us more about your journey."

Inside the big wooden door was an expansive foyer, one with ornate—for Maine—mirrors and a large canvas of sea birds soaring above the coast. Each kid took off their shoes and placed them along the wall.

Lucas took Relle's bag and placed it on a table at the bottom of the staircase with a gleaming wood railing that Sylvia had them polish once a week.

The dining room, like most of the rooms, had a fireplace taller than Gabe. And twenty chairs were placed around an enormous dark wooden table.

"Sit here, Relle," Wynnie said, and Relle did. The young kids fought for a seat next to the new girl, and Mason, a ten-year-old, won. He beamed. Gabe managed to get a spot across from them, and Relle told her story.

"The summer the world ended"—she nodded at Gabe when she said it—her schools had closed immediately. Her parents were instructed to stay home too. When their cheeks bloomed with the rash, she called the ambulance. No one showed up, so she ran to her neighbors. She couldn't find anyone. Relle didn't want to talk too much about that part, and so she didn't. She skipped ahead and told them about the library caving in and how

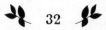

she decided she would go to Maine, because she thought maybe it was far enough away, maybe the air was clear and there would be people.

For the most part, the other children didn't bring up the last days either, or the week when they'd tried to contact their homes and families. No one wanted to remember that part.

Gabe ate his pasta while she spoke. He was sick of pasta for lunch, but pasta lasted forever. He would probably have to eat pasta for lunch for the rest of his life. He missed food from the grocery store, like avocados and bananas. Kiwis. He couldn't even remember their taste.

When he was in elementary school, Before, his mother would eat lunch with him once a week. Parents were allowed to join them whenever they wanted, and they'd sit on a little platform in the cafeteria. All the other kids would be envious of the fast food the parents brought.

He wanted fries and a burger from a fast-food restaurant. He'd take a flat patty from McDonald's or, even better, the one from his favorite place that came rolled up in tin foil with pickles and mayonnaise and cheese. They rarely ate meat now, and he missed it. He liked fresh fish and lobster and clams, but sometimes he wanted something that dripped down his hands with grease.

At least there was bread. Homemade bread was good.

Gabe looked at Relle occasionally. He didn't want to look too much. He didn't know why he felt that way. Everyone else couldn't take their eyes off her and her sad story.

The spell hadn't worn off. If he believed in magic, which he didn't, he would have thought she'd slipped them a potion. But he was too sensible for that.

He didn't blame the other kids for their fixation. She was a good storyteller, and they were all desperate for someone new. Her eyes were big, and her face was animated. She used her hands a lot. Gabe finished his pasta while she performed, her plate barely touched.

Usually after lunch, they worked on school individually. Nora Andrews, who was twenty-two and the oldest of the kids, would put the youngest down for naps or quiet time, while Sylvia worked with the elementary-age students. Gabe and the other teens learned and read on their own. The library was big, and they'd added books from the mainland and big island libraries during supply runs.

For the last few weeks, Gabe had been reading a science textbook and a homeopathy book with lots of old pictures. He thought it was the most practical thing to learn, and it had helped him when Bear had broken his arm in January slipping on ice. It was all healed now. He was proud of that.

Sylvia, knowing they wouldn't actually do any studying that day, told Violet and Wynnie to show Relle to her room. She would share with them. And then the others could take her around the island on a tour.

Gabe waited with the boys in the living room off the front foyer. There were multiple living rooms. His home wasn't anything like this mansion. His house on the big island was smaller. He closed his eyes and thought of the warm kitchen with the woodstove and the cramped backyard. He didn't know if it still looked the same. He was too scared to ask.

Eric and Nora would go back often to get supplies. Pasta and rice from the restaurants and school. The hardware store when they needed caulk or paint. The pharmacy for over-the-counter medicine and Band-Aids. It wasn't like how the movies showed the end of the world. Nothing had been ransacked.

"She's cute," Malachi said. Gabe's best friend was short and muscular with light brown skin. He was high energy all the time. When they were little, he was the kid doing flips at recess. He still did flips. "Kinda weird, though. Two years out in the wilderness does something

funny to your brain." He scowled. "I would have walked south. Imagine walking toward the cold." Malachi shook his head and shivered with his whole body. "Yeah, Florida, Georgia, somewhere warm."

Gabe couldn't imagine leaving the island. He slung himself over a maroon chair. In the winter, it was his favorite spot near the fire.

"What if she's a murderer?" Eric said. He walked around the others and flicked Lucas's ear.

"What?" Gabe said. "Eric. No." Eric always said stupid stuff.

"But Sylvia was right," Lucas said. "We should probably take down the sign. If Relle survived, who else survived? What if they come after our supplies? Or try to move in or kick us out?"

Gabe was surprised. Lucas was usually very kind and sensitive. He wasn't skeptical.

"I don't know," Gabe said. If more people were alive, maybe life could be like Before. Wouldn't that be a good thing? Maybe there were adults who knew how to make penicillin or set up fast-food restaurants.

"I think we need to do better surveillance," Eric said.

"Maybe," Gabe answered. He didn't want to talk about that. He wanted Relle to come back downstairs.

Malachi and Lucas and Eric argued about guard duty,

about who would be better at it and what they would do to attackers, and Gabe tried to listen to what was happening on the floor above.

There were ten bedrooms in the house, eight on the second floor. That's how big the house was. Above that, on the third, were two more bedrooms, though no one used them, and a gym with fitness equipment. Sometimes he used the weights, but it felt weird when he wasn't training for anything.

He heard kids stomp down the front stairs, and he sat up quickly. *What is wrong with you?* he wondered. *Stop it.* He was embarrassing himself.

Relle and Wynnie and Violet were linked at the arms. "Oh, Wynnie and Violet," Relle said, sighing, "it was even more beautiful than I could have imagined. I cannot wait to room with you. I feel as if I'm in a dream, and I never want to wake."

"That was weird," Lucy said.

Wynnie laughed at their little sister, who was a nightmare, in a good way. Gabe liked Lucy. She reminded him of his little sister, which was both comforting and awful. His own sister would have been twelve this year. It was strange to think of her as twelve and not ten. He had changed so much from fourth grade to sixth, and Caroline would have done the same. Gabe cleared his throat.

"Let's show Relle the island," Violet said.

They all ran back outside, and Gabe followed. He let the little ones go ahead of him, and they locked onto Relle's hands and pulled her to the goats. The goats jumped in the chaos of eighteen, now nineteen, kids. Relle laughed. Gabe smiled.

Bear and Delphine pulled Relle to the barn and the orchard and then finally to the cliffs and rocks on the north side of the island.

And he kept following. He was not used to following. He was usually the one at the front of the line.

Near the cliffs, the older kids made sure the younger ones didn't get too close to the edge. Gabe loosely rested his fingers on Bear's shoulders. The rocks were high, and white water rammed into them, then swirled below. It was dangerous and overwhelming and pretty. From here, all they could see were rocks and water and sky.

Relle turned around, her face flushed, and said, "Oh, I feel as if this is the edge of the world, and I never want to return."

The edge of the world. That was exactly how he felt.

And as if Malachi had punched him as hard as he could, Gabe knew, in the center of his stomach, that he was in love with the weird girl with the red hair.

He was incredibly embarrassed.

Gabe thought being in love, especially when the other person didn't know, was maybe the worst feeling in the world. It had to be. He couldn't think straight. It clogged his brain. When he woke up, Relle. When he was eating breakfast, Relle. When he was mucking out the goat pen, like he was now, Relle. He wouldn't wish it on anyone. Peter asked him a question and Gabe needed him to repeat it four times.

"Ah, it's that new girl, isn't it?" Peter asked. He wiped his hand along his Carhartt coveralls and laughed. "She talks so much, I don't have to say a word." He barely spoke, especially when they were in the big group, but sometimes out in the barn, he would share stories with Gabe.

"What? I don't know what you're talking about," Gabe answered as Peter took the pitchfork from his hand. But they both knew he was lying.

"Might need to do something about it," Peter said.

Gabe grunted as an answer. He wasn't used to talking to Peter about things like this. Yes, Peter had taught him how to skin a rabbit and how to tap a tree in March, but they never talked about feelings.

"I was never good about that," Peter said. "Never told anyone." He waved his hands. "Liked being by myself more than with other people anyway."

"She is a little strange," Gabe said. Because that was easier than admitting a crush. He was sweating and lifted up his shirt to wipe his face. "She has an imaginary friend."

"We all do what we can to get by. Some of us are better at it than others." The man picked up the wheelbarrow full of hay and goat mess. "When I get back, we'll check on the indoor garden. Last frost already happened. Can probably start transferring over the tomatoes next week."

On the fourth day of Gabe's crush, the kids were in the library listening to Sylvia teach history. It was the only class they took together, the young ones and the older kids. It was the morning part of school. Gabe didn't mind school, either before or after the end. He liked listening to Sylvia talk at the front of the room because it reminded him of when life was normal.

But today he was antsy.

He hadn't talked to Relle, not like he had in the ferns or on the boat, since her arrival. They hadn't been paired up for any chores. Not dinner. Not in the garden. Not cleaning. It was torture.

A few feet away, she was sitting with her legs curled beneath her on one of the plush maroon chairs. A book was closed on her lap, and she propped her arm and chin on it. Relle watched Sylvia at the front of the room with a dreamy smile on her face, one that made Gabe think she was not enthralled by the current topic—the War of 1812—but off in a totally separate world.

Gabe wanted to talk to her. Or at least get her attention.

He took his chance with a whisper. "Relle."

When she didn't answer, he tried her other name. "Cecilia."

He was a little embarrassed that he had to try a second time. Like when you thought someone was waving at you, but it was the person behind you. That kind of feeling in his stomach. Gabe knew he had one more chance. And then he would stop and go back to half listening to the violation of U.S. maritime rights.

Gabe leaned close to Relle and the braid that hung over her shoulder. It was bright and shiny and reminded him of the cat on the mainland. The one who never let Gabe get too close. He thought about tapping her on the shoulder. *Was that allowed? Could he touch her?*

Before he could do anything, Relle tipped her head up but kept her eyes on Sylvia. "It's not very polite to stare, Gabe," she whispered.

He scowled. "I wasn't staring." But his heart fluttered when she said his name. Maybe he had been staring.

"Roy said you were." She faced him. "He believes you have romantic intentions."

"Would I have to duel him?" Gabe wasn't sure if he should joke about it or not—the fact that she had an imaginary friend. Also, was his crush that obvious? And did he care if it was obvious? It was all so confusing.

"You would certainly lose if so."

Gabe grinned. "I'm pretty competitive. I might stand a chance." He wanted to spend time with her. They needed something to do together. She hadn't played basketball with them during their free time in the evenings.

Instead, she had gushed over the newest baby goat with Violet while he and Malachi and Wynnie played under the hoop.

"Not as competitive as I am," she said. Her face was very serious. "I mean, not as competitive as Roy is."

"What about Scrabble?" he asked. "Do you know how to play?" After dinner they all went into the biggest living room to play board games and act stupid until Sylvia eventually kicked them out and they ran around the lawn. He usually played with Malachi. Gabe mostly won because Malachi would stop trying halfway through and flirt with Violet or Chloe. He'd plonk down any letter. Gabe was more calculated. He thought about the points on the board first, the word second.

"I have never played Scrabble before, I have to admit. I imagine I would be good at it because of my vocabulary and my time in the library."

He smiled. "After dinner?"

"I will play Scrabble with you after dinner, Gabe Sweeney."

He thought maybe it would clear his head, having a time set aside to hang out with Relle, but it did not. It was all he thought about. He daydreamed about what they would talk about and jokes he would make. Gabe caught himself smiling and distracted while he finished chores—compost duty, possibly the worst chore—the whole time he read medical textbooks, and all through dinner.

The spell had not worn off. It was getting worse.

But it made the day a swift breeze, moving so quickly until it planted him firmly in the now. When the dishes were cleared, he walked with the others into the living room.

When Gabe went to get the board, Wynnie was holding the red box. Wynnie didn't usually play Scrabble. They usually sat in the corner clump of chairs, singing or telling stories or braiding hair.

"Let's all play," Wynnie said.

He liked playing with Wynnie, but not today. Wynnie hadn't been a part of his daydream. But Relle was gazing up at them from the floor like she wanted Wynnie to play. Gabe tried to hide his annoyance. "Okay."

They set up the board. Gabe got a piece of paper and wrote their names at the top to keep score. Malachi flopped on the floor next to Relle and explained the rules to her. Her eyebrows were scrunched in concentration.

They each drew a tile to see who would go first. Gabe's

was blank, which meant it was him. He filled his rack with seven tiles and stared at the letters. He was going to have to pretend Relle wasn't there if he wanted his brain to work. He put down the word *way*. It was short, but the *y* and the *w* gave him a lot of points. Eighteen.

Malachi went next and then Wynnie. And then it was Relle's turn. She formed the word *vote* and got fourteen points.

A little thrill ran up Gabe's spine. He liked competing. A lot. Maybe too much, his sister had thought. He thought she was wrong. He liked it just the right amount. It was her and Mom who always ganged up on him in Uno.

He was excited like it was a real game, like a sport from Before. He leaned forward in his chair and studied the board. Gabe spelled the word *ex*. It gave him fifty points.

Relle pursed her mouth. She put down the word *cove* off of Malachi's word and scored fourteen more points. She beamed at Gabe.

When it was over, and Gabe had won, Relle stood up from the table and looked him in the eye. "Congratulations, Gabe," she said. "I look forward to a rematch as soon as possible."

Gabe was looking forward to it too. So much so, it made him feel dizzy. That night, when he went to sleep, he dreamed of Scrabble letters and freckled smiles and winning matches.

Somewhere in his dream, he realized he hadn't looked forward to anything in a long time.

In the morning, Gabe was as foggy as the little island. Foggy but happier. He woke up to Mud's paw in his side and rubbed his face. "Okay," he told his dog. Gabe pulled on a sweatshirt and slipped on his shoes while she pranced next to him.

The rest of the house was quiet as they went down the stairs and out the big door. He shivered on the porch while his dog sprinted and peed near the snowball bushes that would erupt with white blossoms soon.

He could hear Peter in the barn, and Gabe walked over to talk to him. *I did something about it*, he thought about saying, but did playing Scrabble actually count? Maybe not.

Peter was sawing a piece of wood. It looked like it was part of the garden fence. The old man was sweating from his brow. Gabe frowned. Peter had heart problems, and it was too cool out to be sweating so much.

"Hey, Peter," the boy said.

"Gabe."

"Are you feeling okay?" Gabe asked.

"Fine, fine."

Gabe rubbed the sleep out of his eye. Peter didn't look good. He was leaning heavily against the sawhorse he was working on.

"I could check your blood pressure," Gabe said. He knew how and had done it before. Had told Eric which medications to find from the pharmacy on the big island. "Would you mind?" He felt ridiculous asking. But practically, they needed Peter to be healthy. He ran the farm. Knew how to work all the tools and repair things. Knew how to birth the baby goats in the spring. Knew how and when to plant and harvest the crops that helped keep them all alive.

Besides that, more personally, Sylvia and Peter were . . . well, they weren't exactly parents, but they were the closest thing Gabe had. He'd assumed they would always be on the island. That Peter would show him how to shave his face when it was time. A lump gathered in Gabe's throat.

The old man waved his hand at him, which was as much a yes as Peter would give, so Gabe went back into the house and brought out the medical supplies they had collected.

Gabe had him sit on the sawhorse. He placed Peter's arm in the cuff and pushed the button to start. The number was bad. Gabe scratched his neck. He lightly pressed his index and middle finger to Peter's wrist and counted, his eyes on his watch. Each beat pounded in Gabe's head. *Stop it*, he told himself. *It's fine. He'll be fine.* "Has your chest hurt at all?" he asked.

Peter shook his head both up and down and side to side. Which wasn't really an answer.

Gabe raised his eyebrows and draped the stethoscope around his neck like his father used to do.

"I've got to finish this fence," Peter said.

"You need to rest for a little bit," Gabe said, gently, in his dad's doctor voice. To keep them both calm. His dad had used it when things were bad. He had used it on Gabe before. "I think Eric or Nora could mend the fence, even though you would do a much better job than Eric."

Gabe thought humor was probably part of being a doctor. It made everything seem less dire.

If Peter had had a heart attack Before, he would most likely have had surgery on the mainland. At the big hospital down Route 1, where Gabe had once stayed with pneumonia. But there was no hospital now, and Gabe wasn't qualified to do any type of surgery. Unless stitches counted, and even then.

"I'll take a nap this afternoon," Peter answered.

Gabe did not want to tell an adult he needed more than a nap. He squirmed inwardly, but on the outside, he patted Peter's shoulder. "I know you don't want to, but I need you to go lie down inside. And I'm not the only one who needs you. The rest of the kids do too. We've got a big summer of harvesting everything you planted. We won't be able to do it without you. In a week or two, you can come back out to the barn and fix whatever Eric messed up." Gabe laughed a little. He was faking it.

Peter regarded him. "Gabe . . ."

"I know," Gabe said, though he didn't know. He hoped it was reassuring. He felt very young and very old at the same time. The end of the world had done that. But maybe being fourteen felt like that anyway. He didn't know.

Peter wanted to put up a fight, Gabe could see. He

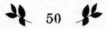

looked like he was debating the outcome. He'd start to say something, stutter, and put the thought back inside his brain.

"A week or two and you'll be as good as new." Gabe didn't know if that was true or not. He felt guilty for the lie. Or the maybe lie, he couldn't know.

Peter nodded and Gabe was relieved. His shoulders dropped. If anything, rest wouldn't hurt at all.

Gabe and Peter walked back toward the house. They were the same height, but one was stooped with age and the other was not fully grown. "I remember your father," Peter said.

Gabe's heart buckled. "Do you?"

"He was a good man," Peter said. He had a habit of saying very few words, but they always meant something. Gabe thought it was the truest, kindest sentence he'd ever heard. It was also a sentence to strive for.

Like he could hear his thoughts, Peter said, "You're a lot like him. Yup."

"I'd like to be." Gabe thought that if only his father were there, maybe everything would be okay. He'd be able to help Peter. He'd help the other kids. He would be able to give him advice on what to do with Relle.

His throat felt full and terrible. He missed him so much. None of it was fair.

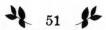

"You're the boy helping an old man to his room. You'll get there."

For a week, Peter stayed in bed. And Gabe read page after page about heart disease. The frustrating part was that nothing was helpful. None of the books had a plan for after the world ended. He could give Peter aspirin, but he couldn't perform angioplasty surgery. He didn't know how to insert a stent. The best he could do was find a holistic medicine manual, and that recommended green tea and magnesium, which he gave to his patient. But there was no change in Peter.

Relle liked to read to Peter in the afternoons, and after that Gabe would check Peter's stats. In the hallway, before he walked in, Gabe liked listening to her voice. It was powerful and full of emotion. When it dipped with sadness, Gabe felt that sadness, and when it roared with indignation, Gabe echoed that rage.

He stepped into the room when she was finished, and both Peter and Relle looked up. She was sitting in the wooden chair next to the window.

"I'll stop by tomorrow," she told Peter. "My favorite

part is next. The dastardly thief is caught by the enchanting princess."

She walked around the bed and Gabe didn't know how people could concentrate when the person they loved was around. He could not.

When she left, he leaned over Peter, listened to his heart and checked his blood pressure. The holistic book said a healthy diet and exercise were important to heart health, but Peter already had those. Gabe pursed his lips. "What if we started with something like thirty minutes of walking a day?"

"Oh, I'd rather do something productive instead," Peter said. "I noticed the step leading down to the cellar was wobbly. Might go fix that."

Gabe sat in the chair. "Hmm," he said. He really didn't like giving Peter directions. First, he wasn't sure of anything. And second, it felt strange to lecture an adult. "Okay, I'll make a deal with you. Fix the step, but if it takes longer than thirty minutes, you let one of us finish it." He thought that sounded fair.

Peter coughed, then nodded. "You know," Peter started, "Relle is a real bright thing."

"She is," Gabe agreed. He stood up, gathering the medical supplies and pushing the chair back. It scraped across the wood floor. "She's very good at Scrabble."

Peter laughed. "She does have a way with words."

"I think probably she'll beat me soon." And he both wanted that to happen and didn't want that to happen, which felt good.

"Better get a dictionary and start studying, then."

Gabe smiled and wrapped the stethoscope around his neck. "You know, I haven't really felt like . . . I haven't really felt like myself. Since everything." He scowled. "I haven't felt very competitive, which I know is probably a good thing. I don't know. At least that's what my sister said. But . . ." He sighed. "Playing Scrabble with Relle makes me feel like me."

Peter nodded. "Sometimes it takes a stranger to show us bits of ourselves we didn't know we were missing."

After dinner, when they all went into the living room, Relle was standing at the front, near the fireplace. She was wearing a dress, yellow with small flowers. He didn't recognize it as one of the other girls'. Maybe it was from a box in the attic or someone had brought it over from the big island. Her hair was loose and wavy. Violet and Wynnie stood on each side of her.

"Attention, good people of the island," she said. Her voice was big and animated. "We are proud to announce that next Friday we will commence with the inaugural installment of the . . ." Her eyes went wide. "Talent show."

The kids applauded, and Gabe looked around the room. They were all whispering excitedly. He did not feel as enthusiastic. Would Relle expect him to participate? He didn't exactly have a talent. He couldn't sing or dance. And why was everyone so happy? What was the point of a talent show at the end of the world?

"Get your acts ready!" she demanded. "And if you don't have a talent to showcase, you can be in the play that Lucas and I are writing."

"What're you gonna do, man?" Malachi sat across from him and spread the game board between them. "You gonna play Scrabble?"

Gabe watched Relle clasp hands with Wynnie. She was bright, Gabe agreed with Peter on that. And pretty. It tugged a little on his heart. Was he allowed to feel joy? To feel happiness in the After? It seemed silly in the current circumstances. "I don't know."

"Well, you're not dancing with me. I've seen you dance," Malachi said. "It's not pretty. Got all the rhythm of a mushroom."

"No, definitely like an asparagus," Gabe joked.

"Asparagus? Asparagus!" Malachi stood up like Gabe had insulted him. Flung his arms wide. "This man thinks he's asparagus! Tell him, Bear!"

From across the room, Bear said, "A mushroom," with a little, straight face.

"I could write you a part of a mushroom in the play for the little ones," Relle said, joining them at Scrabble and sitting next to Gabe. "There are dragons and fairies. I don't see why there couldn't be a mushroom."

"Okay," Gabe said, but he really did not want to be in the play with the little ones, did he? She was joking, wasn't she?

He didn't know. They played Scrabble, and her face was intense. She made some new moves. A few quick little two-letter words that didn't seem like much but combined with some of the tougher letters, like *x* and *z*, scored well. He wrote down her scores and tried not to talk. His sister always rolled her eyes if he gave her compliments while they were playing anything. *Stop treating me like you know better!* So he didn't say anything to Relle.

Malachi left halfway through the game to talk to Violet. Wynnie did their usual, small points each round, and Gabe scored triple word points in the corner. But Relle won. Her words were longer and she was using Gabe's strategy, it seemed, to go for the spaces with the highest points on the board first.

"Good game," she said. Her face was very serious.

Gabe did not like losing, usually, but he didn't mind losing to Relle. He thought that was probably love. One Thanksgiving, he remembered his mother yelling in the kitchen that she could peel a potato faster than his father. He didn't remember who won. All he could remember were the potato skins on the floor.

"You too." He smiled. "Tomorrow?"

"Yes." Relle leaned forward and whispered. "Sometimes I'm embarrassed by how much I like winning. But really there is no better feeling than beating a worthy opponent."

Gabe knew exactly what she meant, and he went to sleep content.

In the morning, the kids were talking about the talent show. Wynnie's little sister was going to do stand-up comedy. Lucas was going to play his guitar and sing a song he wrote. Gabe didn't know why everyone was so excited. It was all stuff they already did. Lucas already played his guitar and sang. Lucy already told jokes all the time.

But he felt happy. After breakfast, he whistled up the great stairs to the second floor to check on Peter. He was eager to tell him about Scrabble and get the older man's

advice on the talent show. First, he waited outside the big bathroom so he could get his supplies, and when Chloe *finally* came out, he grabbed his stethoscope and the cuff.

Gabe was confident. He whistled across the hallway. Maybe he'd tell Relle he liked her. Maybe Peter would help him find the right words.

He stepped through the doorway to the small bedroom next to the stairs. Peter's. He scanned the white room. Sylvia was there. She picked her head up and wiped her eyes. The bed behind her was empty. Stripped of its bedding, so the blue mattress showed bare. With no Peter that Gabe could see.

Gabe stopped. Stopped whistling. Stopped walking. Stopped everything.

"Is Peter feeling better?" he asked.

Time froze, then sped up, double-timed. *Where was Peter?* Maybe he'd missed him somehow. Maybe he'd catch movement out of the corner of his eye. Or maybe he was out in the barn.

"Gabriel," Sylvia said.

No one said Gabe's full name. It was his grandfather's name, so it belonged to someone else, a man with bushy eyebrows and a bald head. Gabe wasn't even sure how Sylvia knew that was his name, it was used so infrequently.

Sylvia stepped closer to him. Gabe's body went cold. "Where's Peter?" Gabe whispered. He gripped the doorway. Pressed it so tight his knuckles were white.

"Gabriel," Sylvia said again, and dread ran through Gabe. He immediately thought of the last day on the big island. It rammed into him. He shook his head.

"I was going to check on him. He seemed to be doing better." Gabe was trying to argue with . . . well, death.

"Eric and I . . ." She was very quiet. Sylvia folded her hands together. "Peter was . . . I'm surprised two old birds like us lasted so long." Sylvia attempted a laugh. "We weren't supposed to survive the end of the world."

Gabe did not cry at first. He started shaking. It was something he couldn't control. His hands vibrated and then his arms and his legs and he couldn't stop. He felt Sylvia grasp him.

"You did a good job trying to take care of him, but we do not have the same resources," Sylvia said. Gabe still didn't cry. His throat was hot. His eyes burned. "He needed a hospital. He needed surgery."

Gabe shook his head. No, he should have done something more. Maybe if he hadn't let Peter exercise thirty minutes a day. Gabe felt sick.

"I'll have to tell the others," Sylvia said. She broke apart from him. "We'll gather in the dining room."

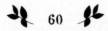

Gabe couldn't. He couldn't face the others. That made him feel like a coward, but he couldn't do it.

That sick feeling pressed on his stomach. On his chest. And his shoulders shook. He moved across the hall and down the stairs as if he were floating. But not floating like a bubble or anything nice. Not floating in the Maine ocean. He was a balloon about to rupture.

Gabe floated across the wide, shining foyer. Through the big door with stained glass. Down the front steps. There, Gabe stopped and bent over. His hands on his knees, he leaned over and tried to catch his breath. To catch himself. To stop the shaking in his hands and arms and body.

"Relax, Sweeney," he said.

He pursed his mouth and sucked in air. Blew it out very intentionally through his nose.

It didn't work. Nothing was going to work.

9

Death and Gabe were well-acquainted.

The end of the world had started in Texas. When the news first reported the new illness, Gabe's father had paid close attention. He was interested in pandemics. The only symptom was vomiting and a bright rash across the cheeks and nose. And some people didn't even get the rash. Gabe's father frowned at the information from the TV. "Wash your hands," he reminded them as they left that morning. "Wear a mask if you go out. If this is anything like the last one, it'll change everything for the next few months."

By the end of the day, officials were recommending schools close until the coast was clear.

Which meant that school was out for the summer. They only had five days left anyway. On their phones, kids rejoiced. *No school! Thank you, Texas!*

It was a joke.

The other kids went to the beach. Gabe had to hear about it online. He begged his mom to let him leave the house. Lacrosse was canceled, and he was bored.

"No, Gabe. The last time this happened, you got sick. I'm not letting it happen again."

His father hadn't left his office on Main Street. He'd had too many patients that day. He'd opened up his doors for all hours. Everyone was too sick to drive to the hospital on the mainland.

On the third day, Gabe's sister threw up. And then his mother. He called his father at the office. "Dad . . ."

On the other end, his father stopped him. "Gabe. I might not make it home tonight."

"Dad?" Gabe choked. Gabe could tell his father didn't just mean he'd sleep at the office like he had been doing.

"There's a woman, Sylvia, who is taking all the healthy people across to the little island, the one the Glovers owned. You know that one? Just until everyone's healthy.

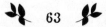

You need to leave now. Head down to the marina, Gabe. Wear a mask. They're in the bathroom."

"I can't."

"You can."

"No." He was crying. Crying harder than he'd ever cried in his life. His feet refused to go to the bathroom to look for masks.

"This is moving faster than anything they've ever seen," his father said. "There's no time for the usual protocol, buddy. No time for quarantines and testing. It'd take months to make a vaccine. You have to, Gabe."

"I don't want to." His voice was wobbly and weak. He couldn't believe it was true. *Was his father lying? He had to be.* Even though he'd never lied to Gabe before.

"Let me talk to your mother," his father said. Gabe heard commotion in the background. "I love you, Gabe. So much."

Gabe ran to the edge of the world. He watched the waves crash against the big rock. He felt like the rocks. And wave after wave was the end of everything normal. End of his family. End of life as he knew it. And now, the end of Peter. They pounded into him.

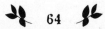

Gabe sobbed. It wasn't fair. None of it was fair. Peter dying. His family. He hated everything. He hated the world and what was left of it. The After was awful. It was terrible and nothing.

He cried and wiped his nose and made noise that was something like talking and something like yelling and none of it made sense. He kept ranting. He missed his sister. He missed her so much. They used to make these stupid pretend worlds on their trampoline and stupid games with jump ropes and everything was stupid and awful.

Gabe wanted to play those stupid pretend games with her. Once, he was a dog barking and she was his owner. Stuff like that. Really, was it fair that he was still here, and she was . . . well, she wasn't. She wasn't here. *Why wasn't she here? Why weren't any of them?* And now Peter wasn't here either.

Gabe felt sick. It was his fault. If he had taken better care of him . . . *Hadn't Peter been the only one who knew when to plant the gardens? Didn't he know the harvesting schedules? How to run the electricity? What would they do without him?* And Peter was kind. He was kind and worked hard and was really nice. He listened when Gabe needed him to listen. *And what had he said about Relle?* He liked Relle.

Relle.

Gabe was embarrassed that Relle was going to find out he had failed. *Wasn't he supposed to be some kind of doctor? Not a doctor, but at least helpful? Didn't the other kids think he was special or at least competent?* He wasn't.

She would be sad. They'd all be sad. And it was going to be Gabe's fault. His stomach ached. He stood up straight. He was going to need to tell them all. Gabe was going to need to apologize for Peter. None of them would forgive him, he knew that. But still. He had to say he was sorry.

Gabe turned to face the house, and the girl with red hair was standing right behind him.

"Relle." His voice was very sad. It was full of more emotion than he wanted it to be. Much more. "I'm sorry," he told her, and his voice leaked all over the rocks and the ocean and the grass. "I'm sorry. If I had done . . . more . . ." And more was too much. His voice broke into thousands of pieces and scattered as far as he could see.

"I'm so sorry, Relle," he said, and he was crying much harder than he wanted to. It was all very bad and very embarrassing. And Relle was crying too. Her face was wet, and her cheeks were red.

He pressed his hands to his face. The island would never forgive him. And he would never forgive himself. Who did he think he was—*his father?*

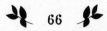

He wasn't nearly as brave. Or smart. Or good.

At the edge of the world, Gabe closed himself like a shell.

And then he felt a hand on his hand. The hand pulled his down. And he felt arms, arms that weren't his own, wrap around his neck. And a head that wasn't his, lean against his.

"It's not your fault," Relle said. "Though I admit Peter's death strikes a blow. It makes me remember all the other death. I imagine it does the same for you. We will probably all feel an immense sadness. I'm sorry you are in the depths of despair."

Gabe nodded against her. Against her hair. He felt the same way. There were no further levels to the despair. They had reached the very bottom. His heart had been plucked out and stomped on two years ago, and any small bits of healing had been tossed aside with Peter now gone.

But here was someone who felt the same way.

His arms were flat at his sides, but Gabe didn't want that. He latched onto Relle as fiercely as she latched onto him. His arms went around her.

At the edge of the world, teetering on the very brink, Gabe Sweeney hugged Relle Douglas. And Relle Douglas hugged Gabe Sweeney.

In the morning, Gabe was not sure what was real and what was imaginary. What was a dream.

He was thirstier than he'd ever been in his life, and he drank glass after glass of water, hoping that it would make the world clear.

It did not.

Peter was gone. That was real. It caused him to cry at the strangest times. He went about his usual morning activities fine and then the reminder of the old man would punch him in the gut and he'd leak tears.

The others were doing the same. Some of them were

brave and cried together. Held on to one another in the living room or the dining room. Wailed when they wanted to. The girls were better at that. At letting their sadness escape. The boys hid it more, and Gabe tried, for the younger ones, not to be embarrassed by the grief.

He hugged little Bear. Patted Mason. Cradled Tim's sweaty, snotty face against him.

But he really wanted to escape.

The one small bright spot, which he hardly dared think was real, was Relle and what had happened by the rocks.

He didn't want to think about it too much. It seemed dangerous. It was nicer than crying, but he felt guilty for the tiny light that sparked inside of him. *Had Relle hugged him? Did he dream it?*

Probably. That was the practical thought, and so he pushed it away.

But he could still feel what it had felt like. Still knew what her hair smelled like. That couldn't be a dream.

Gabe could only battle those two thoughts as he got ready for the funeral. He wore a white button-down shirt and a tie he had tied not really well but not too horribly either. The bathroom was silent except for the drip of the faucet that hadn't been twisted all the way. Gabe turned it off.

When he was finished getting ready, he filed down the stairs with the others and walked outside. The sun shone bright. It seemed rude to shine on such a sad day.

Nora Andrews said a prayer, and Lucas sang a song, his guitar strapped to his chest. It was beautiful and sad, and Gabe let himself feel every note. He watched the green grass under his shoes and let the song run over his heart.

Someone stuck their hand in his. He assumed it was Bear. Gabe gave it a light squeeze and looked at the fingers. They did not belong to a six-year-old. They were Relle's.

She held his hand. *Relax, Sweeney,* he told himself. *You're at a funeral. Maybe you look sad. Maybe she's being kind. It doesn't mean anything else.*

He didn't care. Bravery took over. Gabe ran his thumb over her pinkie nail, his heart stomping louder than the song on Lucas's guitar. Much, much faster. Gabe wasn't sure if what he had done was anything. If it was romantic or friendly or just weird. Or nothing.

No, he decided, it was romantic. He knew he wouldn't have done it to anyone else's pinkie. And he was pretty sure Peter would have approved.

Sylvia made a big lunch. The biggest they'd ever had, but Gabe could barely eat the ham, which they only had on special occasions. Which he was always wishing for. He pushed it around his plate and ate without enjoying it. He couldn't stop thinking about Peter. The entire house was sad because Gabe couldn't save him. He wanted to go to the library and read more. Maybe there was something he'd missed. Maybe the answer was in the books.

But he couldn't leave the table yet. It was his day for cleanup. When everyone was done eating, Gabe picked up the plates and brought them to the kitchen. He separated the scraps into food for the pigs and composting, then emptied the contents into a bucket. He tossed Mud a piece of ham. And Relle walked into the room. She was humming a song from Before that Gabe recognized. One that had played everywhere and too often. The lyrics were terrible. *I couldn't tell you before. But now it's all I can say . . .*

"Do you like that song?" he asked.

She smiled. "I do. It's my very favorite. Don't tell Roy, though, because he hates it."

Gabe did not say he agreed with her imaginary friend. But he did.

"Sylvia said I could make a pie when we're finished cleaning up. Peter loved pie, and I wanted to make one.

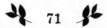

71

In his honor. Apple was his favorite, but I thought I'd use the blueberries you all froze. Do you like pie?" She kept talking. Her cheeks were red, and she rambled about pie as she stacked plates up next to the sink and Gabe. He scraped and rinsed before loading them into the dishwasher.

Was she *nervous*? That idea made Gabe smile. He felt guilty smiling or laughing. It seemed inappropriate after Peter.

"Relle." He turned away from the sink. His shirt was wet where it had brushed the counter. "It's my fault Peter died," he confessed.

She blinked a few times and shook her head. "We talked about this, Gabe. It's not your fault."

"I know." He nodded. He did know. Deep down. "But I *feel* that way."

"There wasn't anything you could do. He was very sick. Sylvia said he needed surgery."

"Yeah, but what if there *were* something I could have done?"

"Like what?" She tipped her head, and Gabe felt very warm and content for a second. And that warmth twisted into guilt.

"I don't know." He sighed and turned back to the dishes. Gabe plunged his hand into the water and scrubbed. It was very quiet except for the washing. He was on the verge of something. So close to grabbing onto an answer. He just didn't know what that answer was.

"Well," she said. "I think the talent show will lift everyone's spirits. We could use some cheering up."

Gabe agreed. In a few weeks, of course she could have the talent show. He wouldn't participate, but he guessed he would watch the others.

"We will have to increase rehearsals soon. There's still so much to do," she said.

"A few weeks is plenty of time to memorize everything," Gabe told her.

"Well, next week," Relle said.

Gabe was confused. "Next week?"

They looked at each other. "Yes. Next week like we planned."

"But . . ." Gabe didn't have the words. "What about Peter?"

"Peter was excited about the talent show. We've been working hard on it. Everyone is excited about it . . ." Her face started to turn red. Her chin stuck out defensively. "I think you're not excited about it, Gabe."

"Can't you postpone it a week or something? Having it so soon is . . . well, it's ridiculous, don't you think?"

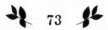

"No, I don't think it's ridiculous," she said. Her voice started to quake. "I do not think celebrating this island and the people on it is *ridiculous*." Her eyes were huge. She looked very upset.

Gabe was upset too. *How could she possibly want to continue with the talent show so soon?* It *was* ridiculous. Besides, there was nothing to celebrate. It was the end of the world. Everyone he cared about was gone. "Reciting poems and dancing around in the living room isn't going to bring Peter back."

"I didn't say it would." Relle's green eyes filled with tears.

Besides his sister, Gabe had never seen a girl cry. Well, that was maybe a lie. But if he had seen them cry, it wasn't because of him. He had never seen the girl he liked cry because of words that came from his mouth. It was horrible. His heart felt like it had been chewed and spit on the ground.

But he was still furious. "You didn't even know him," he said. "Peter was a real person, Relle." His voice shook. "He isn't an imaginary person or something."

Her mouth opened and closed. "I was wrong about you," she whispered. "I thought we would be good friends, Gabe, but I was mistaken. I will never be friends with someone like you. Never." Her voice was flat, which felt very, very wrong to Gabe because usually it was . . . well, whatever the opposite of flat was. Round, maybe. Whole and full of emotion.

He did not care. He was over Relle Douglas.

Three days. They hadn't spoken in three days. When he was around, she gripped Wynnie's hand and marched away in the opposite direction like he didn't exist. He wasn't as dramatic, he didn't think. But he ignored her too.

It was all very frustrating. They weren't even playing Scrabble anymore. Everyone was getting ready for the talent show instead. And while the rest of the island gathered in the living room with papers full of play scripts and spilled into the dining room where the floor was smooth and easy to dance on, Gabe walked to the edge of the world and grumbled to himself, Mud at his side.

Good, he thought, Relle was ridiculous anyway. She wore funny clothes and said words that were too big and didn't make sense and believed in ghosts and fairies and thought having fun was pretending to be a sailor on the high seas. They had nothing in common. He didn't want to talk to her either. She could talk to her imaginary boyfriend or whoever. No, Gabe was done with Relle Douglas and her silliness.

On the fourth day of silence, a Saturday, they all decided it was time to go to the beach for the first time that year, and Sylvia said they were allowed to *if* they wore sunscreen.

They did. Gabe's trunks were red. Malachi's were short and blue. "When your legs look this good, Sweeney, you show 'em off!" They brought a football and passed it back and forth as they walked to the beach. Malachi did dives and one-hand catches like it was the Super Bowl. And he made a lot of noise doing it. It almost distracted Gabe.

Sylvia was at the beach too. She covered the little ones in sunscreen and dug holes in the gritty sand with them. And when they fell asleep because of the sun and the water, she propped an umbrella over them.

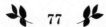

Violet approached Gabe and looked up at him with big eyes. "Do you want to go for a walk with me, Gabe?"

"Well . . ." He knew if he wanted to flirt with Violet he could, but he didn't want to. "I think . . ." And he pointed to his friend until she rolled her eyes and walked away.

Malachi ran into the waves and whooped loudly. He threw his hands in the air. Gabe grinned and stepped toward the water. It was cold. The pebbles and sand numbed Gabe's feet. Malachi waved his hands, and Gabe threw the football right to them.

Yes, he and Relle were too different anyway. He could see her. She and Wynnie and Lucas were building a sandcastle, more like a rock castle. Lucas balanced a small rock on a larger one and raised his arms in triumph.

Lucas had nothing to do with his mood, but Gabe grumbled about his roommate anyway. He could stack more rocks. *She wouldn't like you if you could stack eight thousand rocks*, his sister would have said.

Bam! The football came soaring back to him, and Gabe caught it before it hit his face then tossed it back. This time Malachi ran straight into the water, stretched out flat, and caught the ball, landing horizontally with a smack.

Now Relle had shifted her attention. She lay flat on

her back, eyes closed, on the hard-packed sand. Her arms were folded across her chest like she was dead. The other kids were picking flowers, weeds that grew beyond the grasses, and tossing them on Relle. Gabe did not like it. Not at all. *How could she do that after Peter?*

He cleared his throat and threw the ball over Malachi's left shoulder so Malachi had to jump. He missed and did a flip into the water to get the ball.

Gabe shook his head. Yes, Relle was too weird for him. He did not like her. He did *not*.

Malachi jogged up to him. "Stop staring at your girl. You look weird."

"I'm not." Gabe rolled his eyes. "And she's not my girl. She's . . ."

"Okay." Malachi made a face. "Race you to the rock." And Gabe took off for the water.

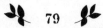

The next day, Malachi didn't come back from scouting on time. He had been gone for four hours. It usually took about two. Sylvia forbade any of them from going after him to the mainland. Just in case. She wanted to wait and not put the rest of the island in danger. No one was allowed near the beach either.

Everyone without kitchen duty climbed to the third floor and stared out the windows with as many binoculars as they could find. There was no trace of their friend. Only the moody Atlantic, the rocky shore, and trees that met the sky. The red post was not visible from the house. The new spring trees had covered it.

Gabe felt anxious. His hands were sweating. He paced around the workout room, on the padded floor, and checked out the window every few minutes. He didn't want to think anything had happened. It was too much. First his family and then Peter. Like pieces of him were breaking off and crumbling into the water. Gabe wasn't sure if he could lose another piece.

No, he told himself, Malachi probably fell asleep. He had fallen asleep at the post before. He fell asleep anytime and anywhere. Sylvia said it was because he was always doing those foolish tricks. He was tired from them. All that carrying on.

As soon as he woke up, he'd bring the kayak back across.

Gabe paced until Lucas cried out, "The boat!"

They all crammed in tight, the youngest on their tip-toes, and watched the kayak push back home to their shore. As soon as they saw Malachi's red T-shirt, they sprinted down the two levels of stairs and headed for the door.

Where Sylvia stopped them short. "It is time for dinner," she said. "Eric and Mason have been working hard. You can wait for Malachi at the table."

Gabe didn't care. It was fine. Everything was fine. Malachi was okay! He sat and waited, both for the food and his friend.

"There are survivors, two of them," Malachi announced, when he came in. "Not survivors like Relle. Like not good guys. They . . ." Malachi twisted his hair. "They felt a little off. I think because they weren't kids. They said they got kicked out of the military base down in Massachusetts. Or left. Or escaped. I don't know. So I thought maybe you wouldn't want 'em around the kids, Sylvia, if they had been trouble. Like what did they do, you know? So I told 'em I was going to get my four-wheeler. I said we had a long journey and to wait there." Malachi bounced on his toes and threw his hands around as he spoke.

"I didn't want to get in the kayak and lead 'em to you. And at this point they were mad. Really mad. And hungry. I gave them the cooler. Guess that wasn't enough. So I ran about a mile down the road, looped back around by the shore, in the brush, and climbed a tree and waited

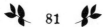

until they left. They waited a long time at the post. I couldn't get the kayak until they went off looking for me. That's when I came home."

"You were very brave, Malachi," Sylvia said. "Very brave and clever."

"Do you think, maybe, they were following me?" Relle asked. "That I accidentally led them all to you? I thought I had simply *imagined* two people following me, but now I think they were real."

"You did nothing wrong," Sylvia said. But she frowned. "We will stop the day trips to the mainland for a while. No one is to travel to the beach until we are certain the men have moved on. No more fires either."

Everyone groaned. The beach was the best part about the island. But Gabe assumed Sylvia wanted to protect them and their house, their resources.

"I know that military base from Before," Relle said. "It's not far from Lowell. I've visited the towns around it for swim meets and farmers markets. Some of my friends' parents worked on it." She frowned. "I never even thought to check if there were survivors there."

There were more survivors. It was both exciting and terrifying. Could life go back to normal? Was it possible?

12

For the rest of the day, it was all they talked about. *More survivors? How many were there? And how had they survived? Had there been a bunker? A vaccine? And if they had escaped the virus, who else had?* It made Gabe's brain move frantically. When it was supposed to be silent study, Malachi recounted the story with bigger movements and gestures, Gabe pulled out a map. It was a book with a laminated cover of New England. He flipped through and found Lowell, Massachusetts, and read the names of the towns around it.

He dragged his finger south and found the base. A thrill ran through him. Right under his finger, there were people. Maybe people who could fix things. People who had medicine and could have helped Peter. Gabe flipped more and found the island. Using the mileage on the side, he connected the two. If he took Route 1 to 95, it was about one hundred miles. One hundred miles to a whole town of people.

He needed to go. He owed it to Peter. There had to be a doctor on the base. Had to be a nurse. *Someone.* And besides, there was nothing on the little island for him.

Gabe waited until the little ones were asleep and the older kids were all in their bedrooms. He knocked on what used to be the park manager's office. Sylvia told him to come in, and when he walked into the room, he saw she had her fingers pressed to her eyes. Gabe imagined it was tiring, watching all of them. And now without Peter.

"Can I go?" he asked. "Can I go to the military base?"

Sylvia opened her eyes and dropped her hands. "Why would you do that?" she asked him. She was much more relaxed at the beach with the little ones, Gabe knew. "You're safe here."

Gabe's heart pounded. "It's not far, a few days. What if there's a doctor? We could have—" He tried to answer. "Maybe Peter would be alive."

"Peter was very old, Gabe."

"Okay, but if someone needs surgery. Or just to see that other people survived!" He didn't want to argue with her. He felt guilty. And rude. She had taken care of them for two years. Of kids who weren't her own.

"I only care about the people on this island now," she said.

"Me too. That's why I need to go."

"You haven't left the island this whole time. Not once."

Gabe nodded and bit his lip. "Sylvia, if you don't let me go, I'll leave anyway." He was very quiet. He would sneak out. He would run away. He would take Mud and run. Whatever he had to do. Gabe didn't often get in trouble, but sometimes it was necessary. He hoped she'd forgive him. "It'll be like two weeks."

Sylvia regarded him. It was something she did a lot. She let the kids figure it out while she watched them. Gabe's parents had done the same thing. He knew he couldn't back down, so he waited her out.

"Well, you can't go by yourself," she told him.

In the morning, Gabe was focused as he pulled on his boots for chicken duty. He hadn't left the island, other than for scouting, in two years. There hadn't been a reason to. Now he had a purpose.

Before, it would have taken a few hours to get to that part of Massachusetts by car. His father sometimes went for work, toured hospitals, that sort of thing, and the whole family would go. They'd visit the museums and Boston Common. There were always so many people. The traffic was awful. Not like Maine. Maine only had traffic when the tourists came.

Gabe whistled as he went out to the barn. He gave the chickens clean water and feed and took the eggs from inside the boxes. Sometimes the hens hid them, so he looked in their favorite spots too. Marietta, a black-and-white Barred Rock, liked to nest in the corner on the ground.

On his way out, Gabe kept the door open so they could roam for the day. The chickens ate bugs and ticks and kept the island clean. Inside the house, Gabe wiped the eggs that had poop on them. It was gross, but chickens were kind of gross in general. He put the eggs in the fridge. Lucas and Chloe were getting breakfast ready for everyone. Oatmeal, which they ate a lot of, and raisins.

He sat down first at the table, and when the others joined him, Sylvia spoke. "Gabe will be going to the base to see if there are any medical professionals. It would be a comfort in emergencies." She waited for everyone to react, which they did, loudly. Sylvia raised her hands. "He will need someone to travel with him. You have all shown yourselves to be helpful and resourceful, like Malachi was yesterday. If you would like to be considered for traveling to the base, please write down your name. Twelve and over only."

"Thank God I'm not old enough," Lucy said. "I hate walking. That sounds terrible."

Sylvia passed out paper and pens. A bowl traveled around the table and the kids placed their names in it. Malachi, Lucas, Nora, Chloe, Wynnie. Relle did not. She crossed her arms. Gabe winced. They would never be friends again.

Fine.

Sylvia stuck her hand in the bowl and pulled out a paper. "Wynnie." She smoothed the paper on the table. "You will accompany Gabe. You may leave tomorrow morning."

Relle started crying. And then Violet starting crying. And then little Bear cried too. After breakfast, he

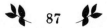

followed Gabe upstairs, to the room Gabe shared with Lucas and Malachi.

Gabe walked into the big closet and pulled out the wool sweater, navy blue and ribbed, that used to belong to his father. It was too big, but it smelled like him. And as much as Gabe had teased him about Maine and L.L.Bean and his dad clothes, the fabric didn't fall apart like some of the other brands.

"Gabe," Bear said. He was holding a stuffed dinosaur. Nora had just given him a haircut, and his ears stuck out in a sweet way. "I don't want you to go. What if you die? What if they shoot you?"

Gabe squatted down to be eye level with Bear. "I'm not gonna die." Though he couldn't quite know. "Well, I . . . I don't know. Someone has to go see if there are more people out there. I guess I'll just have to be brave."

"I wish someone else would go."

Gabe put his hand on the little boy's head. "I know, buddy." He hugged Bear. Gabe's dad had hugged him a lot. "Want to help me pack?"

The six-year-old's words planted a seed of doubt deep inside Gabe. *What if he did die?* He still had things to sort out.

In the movies, in the apocalypse, people somehow knew it was the end of the world. They called their families. They professed their truest loves. In real life, everything felt temporary. Like life would go back to normal in a week at the most. The goodbye to his mother and sister had been so rushed. He would see his family when they were all better. When he left with Sylvia and the others, he didn't know it was the last time he would see them. If he could do it over again, he would have told them . . . well, if he was going to die on this trip, he needed to talk to Relle.

Gabe took back any grumbling about her he had done. Okay, she was a little strange. That was fine. He still liked her. He liked her hair and the way she talked and how she saw the world. *Why was he pretending he didn't?* He was so stupid.

He decided to write her a note. In the afternoon, when he was supposed to be reading in the library, he wrote five rough drafts before it sounded even halfway right. The shorter the better, he figured. And he would *not* say anything about the talent show, even if he did still think it was ridiculous.

I'm sorry about what happened. I hope you can forgive me someday. I like you a lot. I think you're really smart, and playing Scrabble with you is my favorite part of the day. Don't practice too much while I'm gone.

Gabe

He did not say, *If I die, I wanted you to know.* That would be too strange. Even for Relle. Or maybe it would be just the right amount of strange. He didn't know. He stared at the note, trying to figure out if it was a terrible idea. All of it. *Did he have to specify what exactly he meant by like? Or would she know?* He put a little heart above his name.

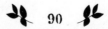

And then groaned out loud.

He almost ripped the whole thing up.

"Wynnie!" he yelled before he chickened out.

The whole room stared at him. Malachi startled awake.

"Sorry," he whispered.

Wynnie walked over, quiet, and hissed, "What do you want, Sweeney?"

"CanyougivethistoRelle?" he spit out, and then he stood up fast, put his book back on the shelf, and walked out of the room as calmly as he possibly could.

The boy put it out of his mind. He had done what he needed to do, and now it wasn't up to him. If she wanted to talk to him, she could. He wouldn't dwell on it. In the morning, he rose early, but Sylvia was already up, cooking. She shooed him out of the kitchen but gave him coffee. He liked it with sugar and the powdered creamer from the big island.

He took it down to the barn. He thought there would maybe be a compass, and even though he didn't know how to use one, Gabe wanted to check. He could figure it out.

Before, Gabe had been fascinated with "end of the world" movies, and his mother let him watch them. She

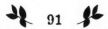

liked them too. When he was in second grade, they rented a new one every day. They made popcorn and camped out in the living room. His favorites involved zombies. He liked when the zombies became people again. Or when the zombies were finished. And when he got to listen to grown-ups swear. His mother's favorites had female characters as the heroes.

"Don't you think this is too mature for him?" his dad asked. "It's kind of violent."

"I don't know," his mom said. "We talk about how it's not real. How it's just a story. We do a lot of survival problem-solving. And we look up if the dog dies before we start."

"Does it?"

"Not in this one."

"I would want an ax," Gabe said. "I'd always carry an ax and a tarp if it were the end of the world. What would you take, Dad?"

"Well, I'd be with you," his father said. "What else would we need?"

They weren't with him.

The barn was empty. Very empty. An old man was supposed to be here, either organizing tools or sweeping, or what Gabe's mother used to call "piddling around." But Peter wasn't there. Gabe pressed his eyes closed and sighed. When he was ready, he opened them and scanned the neat shelves. He found a compass of dark green plastic. When he flipped open the top, a needle danced.

Gabe grabbed the scout hunting knife too. They weren't sending anyone to the post now because of the men Malachi had found. The knife was heavy in his hands. His eight-year-old self would have wanted an ax instead, but they needed protection. Just in case.

He walked back to the house, wanting a kind voice to wish him luck or tell him he was brave. Something.

His bag was packed and by the door. It was a hiking pack, and in it, he had placed clothes and toiletries as well as dried food and peanut butter, a packable hammock, water-purifying tablets and a metal water bottle, and a jar of blueberry jam that Sylvia had wrapped neatly as a gift for the people they might meet. Dog food for Mud. Wynnie had a smaller, folded map of New England. They would walk like twenty miles a day.

He was excited. And nervous. At breakfast, the kids were quiet. They shot glances at him and Wynnie. Lucy cried about her sibling, who patted her hand. And Relle looked like she had spent the whole night wailing, her

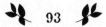

face puffy and serious. She didn't look at him or mention the letter.

Sylvia made eggs and biscuits and goat cheese. She forced him to eat. That's how he knew she cared about them, by when she made them eat. When she filled their plates with more food than they could stomach. But he ate it anyway. He didn't know how long it would be before he would eat warm food again.

"What if there are zombies?" someone asked. Tim, the youngest Andrews.

"There's no such thing as zombies," Sylvia said.

"Relle said there were!" Delphine said.

"I was telling a *story*," Relle said. "You told me you were old enough to hear scary stories, remember, Delphine? Though I admit I had a difficult time sleeping after that one. I scared myself." Relle shivered, and Gabe felt a smile bubble up. She was wonderful.

After they ate, Gabe went to the bathroom, another thing he would deal without—a toilet—and washed up. He looked at himself in the mirror. His dad looked back. Dark wavy hair that Malachi cut for him when he needed it and hazel eyes. "Okay," Gabe said. "Let's do this." He whistled for his dog.

Everyone was outside. They'd formed a line that curved around the driveway. Gabe grabbed his pack and looped it around his shoulders. It was heavy. He said goodbye down the line—Bear was the hardest—and Wynnie did the same. When he stood in front of Relle, she tipped her chin like he barely existed and ran at Wynnie, latching on like a grieving widow. Gabe cleared his throat. He wanted that reaction from Relle. *Had she even read his letter?*

Gabe shook his head and kept moving. At the end of the line was Sylvia.

"Don't be rude to anyone," she said. "Don't make any foolish decisions. Don't forget to drink water, and don't drink dirty water." She was scowling and her arms were pulled close to her.

"Yes, Sylvia."

Sylvia locked him in an awkward hug. "You be good," she said. And then quieter, "You're a good boy, Gabe Sweeney." And that filled him up to almost whole. That little bit.

And then he and Wynnie and Mud were off, down the wide green lawn, through the Avenue, and then onto the beach.

14

They were mostly silent as they rowed across to the mainland. Gabe, his back to the shore, rowed, and Wynnie used the binoculars to watch for the two survivors Malachi had seen. Mud was excited and ran from the front of the boat to the back over and over. She knew they were going on an adventure.

When they hit the rocky beach, they pulled the boat up and hid it under the cover of bushes. Gabe stood back to see if they had been successful. He tipped his head to the side. It was hard to spot the white of the wood.

Gabe and Wynnie followed the same route he had

taken the day he met Relle. But this time, they continued on, down the real road. Route 1. He hadn't left the island in so long. It felt like a different life.

They passed a tire shop and restaurant that had served seafood. Mud peed in the overgrown public park where Gabe had played soccer against the rival team, the Mariners.

A mile up was the McDonald's and a gas station for the highway. Both buildings had been ransacked. Glass broken and pumps knocked over. Abandoned vehicles. A truck with multiple embarrassing stickers on the bumper. His dad would have hated them.

A trash can rolled in the wind. It made a creepy noise that Gabe didn't like. It felt empty compared to the island, which was full of life.

"I don't like this," Wynnie said.

"Me neither."

"Let's get on the highway."

"Yeah, okay."

The highway had more cars. A flipped over Jeep. The people had been traveling in both directions, northeast and southwest. Gabe didn't know where they had been going. Maybe they hadn't either. Either they'd been heading to a specific destination or they had just been trying to get away.

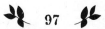

Briefly, after the evacuation, Gabe had felt lucky. Grateful he had survived. And then, it was like winter creeping in. He didn't know *why* he had survived. Not how, though he wondered that too. But *why* had they and not others? Of all the possible people on Earth. None of it made sense.

Survivor's guilt, it was called. Gabe had read about it last winter. It was part of PTSD. It happened a lot when people survived traumatic events. Having a name for it didn't make it easier.

Some of the others felt the same way. Some of them prayed it away. Some of them didn't talk about it at all. Some of them thought they were special, and that's why they had been spared.

Gabe didn't know.

Sylvia was practical about it. "We're here, so we might as well be here."

Gabe wondered what Relle thought the reason was. He bet it was a good one. He'd have to ask her, if she ever talked to him again.

Ahead of him, Wynnie maneuvered in between two luxury cars. "I like this one," they said. "This is the car I would have wanted."

It was bright red. Gabe wondered where the sports car had come from. Maybe Portland, but probably Boston, he figured. The big island was so small and so practical that

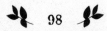

most people only had one car. If they splurged, it was on their boats.

"I wanted a Jeep," Gabe said. "A white one with a tan interior."

The cars cleared out a few miles outside of town. The open highway was bare and boring. Sometimes a fat snake stretched out in the sunshine or a deer flitted off into the bushes. But mostly it was quiet.

They made it twenty-five miles, over pavement and the weeds that poked through, as the June sun blinked hot above them. It would set soon.

"Relle told me she used to sleep outside the most," Wynnie said. "That there were too many ghosts in build-ings." They laughed. "But that there was 'more time to be imaginative outdoors anyway.'"

Gabe laughed too. It made him miss her, and he imme-diately regretted pretending to himself that he didn't care about her. "Did she? She says funny stuff without mean-ing it to be funny."

"Yeah," Wynnie said. "I really like her. I'm glad you found her."

They came across a gas station and decided to sleep there. Gabe pushed open the door, which had been barri-caded. He wasn't sore yet, but he knew he would be after walking all day and sleeping on concrete.

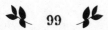

"When are you gonna ask me?" Wynnie said. "You know you want to."

"Ask what?" Gabe rummaged on the shelves. There were old bags of potato chips, salt and vinegar flavored. He opened one. It smelled okay.

"Oh, you think you're so cool," Wynnie said. "I like that Relle Douglas makes you nervous. You never get nervous, so I find it highly amusing that the little red-haired girl makes you all weird." Wynnie stole a chip from him. "Remember when you like saved that baby goat in the spring?" Wynnie wiggled their arms and imitated Gabe. "*Oh, I'm Gabe. I'm so cool and everyone likes me. The girls and half the boys have crushes on me because I'm so cool.*"

"I am not," he laughed. But he was kind of proud of the joke.

Wynnie rolled their eyes. "You're the worst," they said.

Gabe didn't answer. He made a face and said, "Fine! Did you give her the letter? What'd she say?"

Wynnie shrugged.

"Why are you doing this to me? I thought we were friends!"

They were friends. Friends were awful sometimes.

Wynnie stole another chip. "I gave her the letter. She read it. Her face got really red. Redder than usual. And

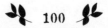

then she folded it back up and did not mention one word to me."

"She didn't volunteer to come with me."

"That's because she's been walking for years. She didn't want to go explore. It's not all about you, Sweeney." Wynnie walked around the gas station. They opened the drink coolers. "Remember when it would be hot outside and the glass doors would open up and the air inside would be so nice and cool? And you would beg your mom to let you get a Gatorade or something and then she wouldn't but sometimes she would. That was the best."

Gabe ignored the coolers. "She read it." That was the important part. That she read it.

"Yeah. She doesn't talk about you. Literally anything else she will go on and on and on about, but not you, Sweeney. Too bad." Wynnie was teasing him.

"It could have been worse." Gabe grinned. "She could have ripped it into five million pieces or chewed it up or done a spell with it over the cliffs."

"She could still do that. Maybe she was saving it for when you were gone."

"Oh yeah." But Gabe smiled again. Maybe Relle didn't quite hate him. Maybe the note had worked. He patted his dog.

Gabe found a broom in the supply closet and swept the floor near the hot dog roller and foam cups. They rolled out their beds. Gabe knew it would get cold at night, with the Maine darkness, and the cement floor, and he put his dad's sweater on before he went to sleep.

In a few days, they'd be with people. More survivors.

And maybe the world would feel normal again.

15

Gabe woke up before Wynnie. They were sleeping, mouth open, their hair all over the floor. He went outside, where it was cold and bright. The fields of grass were wet with dew. Birds chattered on phone lines. He peed behind the building. Mud did the same.

Inside, he looked for supplies as quietly as possible and found some candy bars and a roll of toilet paper. He sat down and read a magazine close to the windows for light. It was *Men's Health*. There were articles about how to get muscles that pop, ads for deodorant, and a spotlight on a rapper who wasn't cool even two years ago.

He flipped through half of it and flung it to the side. There were newspapers, but he didn't want to look. It would be too weird. He knew the pandemic would be the front page. Instead, he rifled through the keychains and lottery tickets and chargers. He scratched one and won two dollars. Behind the counter, the cash register was closed. He pushed the button and the drawer popped open, revealing green bills and metal coins.

Gabe waited for Wynnie to wake up. He hummed to himself, a pop song from Before. He did both parts, the girl singer and the boy. The girl was the one Relle had had a crush on. She had been pretty with short hair. Gabe wondered if she was alive. He wondered if all the famous people were alive and in California still. They had to have survived. Even the rapper from the article. *Didn't they have some sort of rich people protection from the apocalypse?*

Gabe looked at his watch. It was late, and they needed to leave if they wanted to get twenty miles in. He woke up Wynnie with a loud fake cough.

"How long have you been awake?" they asked.

"Umm, two hours."

"I'm sore." Wynnie sat up, their dark hair wild.

"Me too."

"Okay, let's go."

They packed up their stuff. Gabe took another bag of

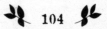

chips and put it in his bag. He fed Mud, then brushed his teeth in front of the mirror and spit out the toothpaste in the sink. Flushed it down with a drip of water from his bottle. Just to be polite to Wynnie, who used it after him.

Gabe's feet marched along at the same beat that they had the day before. Wynnie had a blister, but a Band-Aid too. They were patched up and wearing two pairs of socks. The two of them walked maybe five miles before they talked.

"Remember first grade?" Wynnie asked.

"Yeah." It was a game they played when they were really bored. Gabe picked up a stick and threw it into the weeds that crept over the road. Their teacher had been really pretty and nice.

"Remember when you sang that song to me at that party?" Wynnie laughed. "I just dreamed about it. You were so in love with me."

Gabe laughed. He had been. He'd sung to Wynnie at a classroom party that fall, and the teachers had recorded it and sent it to his parents. They thought his romantic gesture was so sweet.

Wynnie teased him and sang the song. They crooned it. Made it big. Gabe joined in, but he was pretty sure he didn't hit any of the notes. The two of them yelled it loud.

Up ahead, the world looked different.

Gabe stopped. "What is that?" he asked, and he peered through his binoculars. Wynnie stopped singing.

Everything was burnt. A fire. Not recent maybe, but not that long ago. It was a half mile away. Everything looked gray and black. The grass was ashy dirt. Trees reduced to dark stumps. Any branches left were bare and charred.

When they reached it, Gabe and Wynnie both paused. On one side of the line, life, and on the other, death. They had to walk through it, it was the only road, and Gabe felt a creep of apprehension curl up around him. Mud sniffed the ground and padded gently.

"I don't like this," Gabe said. He placed one boot in the ashes. He wanted to get through it as quickly as possible.

"I don't like it either," Wynnie said. "Did you think I'd like the dead road?"

Gabe smiled, but then got serious. "What do you think happened?"

"A fire," Wynnie said. They both laughed.

The only sound was their boots on what was left. Ash. Charcoal. Dust. Gabe took a bandana out of his pack and wrapped it around his face like a mask.

"You look stupid," Wynnie said, but they did the same thing with a shirt.

The fire lasted a mile. A mile of destruction, with no

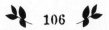

firefighters and trucks spewing water. But then it just stopped. It was green on the other side. *Had it rained? The wind shifted? The fire lost momentum?* Gabe didn't know. He was just glad to be out of it.

They were almost in Kennebunkport. A layer of dust coated everything. They shook their clothes. Gabe wiped off, then drank from his water bottle. It was almost empty, and they'd have to get more. He ate a granola bar from the gas station as Wynnie got out the map. They smoothed it on their thigh and pointed at the roads.

"It looks like we could stay on Route One or go more inside, away from the coast," they said. "It would take the same amount of time."

"Hmm," Gabe said. He followed their finger. The granola bar was sticky and sweet with chunks of dried fruit that stuck in his teeth. "I'd rather stay on the coast." It felt less eerie. More normal. And if they didn't need to use the compass that he wasn't confident about operating, then he didn't want to. Best to follow the highways.

"Me too," Wynnie said. "Who knows what creeps are in the woods."

Gabe had heard about preppers, people who prepared for the apocalypse. They'd stored food underground or in bunkers. They knew how to live off the land or bought enough canned goods to last them a few years.

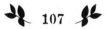

Gabe didn't want to meet any of them in the wilderness. After the men Malachi had found, he was worried that travelers would be desperate and scared. All he and Wynnie had for protection were two knives. The fewer people the better.

For two days, they kept walking, and the towns ticked by. Ogunquit. Bald Head and a fresh stream where they filled their water bottles and used the purification tablets. York. Kittery, where the outlet malls were.

"Can we go?" Wynnie asked. "I want to look."

It was getting late. They'd need to find someplace to sleep soon. But maybe they could camp in one of the stores.

The parking lots had some cars, not many. And a few of the stores had flooded. Gabe guessed it was the sprinkler system. Or burst pipes. Or a hole in the roof. Peter would have known. Windows were broken. One car had driven through an Old Navy, and only the trunk showed. Gabe didn't want to know what animals were living in there now.

But the door for Columbia was unlocked, like whoever was working had stepped out for a bit, and he and Wynnie went in like they were shopping for outdoor gear before the summer the world ended. A large kayak was suspended from the ceiling.

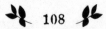

"Too bad we can't carry that back with us," Gabe said. It was bigger than the one down by the beach.

"Let's try on clothes!" Wynnie said, and then did. They carried stacks of clothes to the changing rooms and yelled out comments. Gabe laughed when his friend twirled in front of the mirror. He walked around the store and swapped out his rain jacket for a lightweight cloud-colored one. And a few pairs of socks. His own smelled bad from all the walking.

Outside, they found a fountain full of rainwater. Mud jumped in it, and Gabe had to wrestle her out. He found a pair of sunglasses at a sunglasses store, and Wynnie got a designer purse with hearts all over it.

"What do you want that for?" Gabe asked.

"Just let me enjoy this, Gabe!"

Back inside the first store, they pulled all the sleeping bags off the rack and piled them up high in the display tent. Gabe and Wynnie fell asleep as soon as they closed their eyes. And Mud curled between them.

16

In the morning, they walked across two bridges, the wind pushing them along like it wanted them to get to the base faster. Big ships rested in the shipyard. Some tethered. Others not. All clumped together like rubber ducks at a carnival. One had not survived. Its bow rested at the bottom of the harbor, the other end pointing awkwardly at the gray sky.

It was cold out, and Gabe layered his new jacket over his dad's sweater so the wind wouldn't cut through him. They walked on toward Hampton Beach. The cheesy boardwalk with bright colors had faded, and the air no longer smelled like board fries and fried seafood. Gabe had been there for the annual sandcastle competition, where artists carved great works of art into mounds of sand. They weren't there now, the sandcastles, but it was still pretty. They stood on the beach and carved their names into the sand. *Gabe Was Here. Wynnie Hogan for President of the World!*

The coast of New Hampshire was short, and they traveled into Massachusetts by the afternoon. The three of them slept in a barn. It was the worst night of sleep they'd had. Gabe wished they were back in the store. That had been nice. Almost as nice as the big bed on the island.

In the morning, Gabe smelled terrible. Just awful. It was the barn and not bathing for a few days and the ash of the fire. On the island, they had a schedule and each kid ended up in the bath or shower, run by well water, a few times a week. Which, Before, would have been kind of gross, but now was probably the best they were going to get.

"I'm going to jump in that pond," Gabe told Wynnie.

He didn't want to. He knew the water would be cold. He groaned as he walked outside. He had nice soap, fresh-smelling citrus like oranges or maybe grapefruit, from one of the shops at the outlet mall. Gabe stood on the edge of the pond and stared at the water. He hoped there weren't leeches.

Better do it fast, he told himself. His muscles were already tense. He pulled his arms out of his sleeves but left them in the chest of his sweater like it was a poncho or something.

"Okay, Sweeney," he whispered.

Gabe undressed quickly and closed his eyes. He plunged into the water and clenched every muscle. The cold slammed into his chest. He popped up and gasped. Whooped loudly at the shock.

His hands were vibrating as he poured the soap into his palm. "It's so cold!" he yelled. He rubbed his hands together and scrubbed his head and body as quickly as he could while kicking his legs to stay on the surface. He dunked again, and this time he was ready for it.

When he was finished, Gabe crawled out and got dressed as fast as his shaking fingers would let him. He didn't towel off. There was no towel. And he walked, cold and exhilarated, back to the barn. He felt clean and smelled good.

"You're very dramatic," Wynnie said.

But Wynnie whooped even louder when they jumped in, Gabe heard from inside the barn. He couldn't wait to rub it in.

They woke up on the fifth day with seventeen miles to go. If they hurried, they could be at the base by nighttime. And then they could maybe sleep in a bed or cot. Or whatever they had. It was better than a barn and a pond. Gabe daydreamed as he walked. He imagined the base was exactly like the world used to be, but better somehow. He played out entering the gates, the soldiers delighted there were more survivors.

The people cheered for Gabe and Wynnie, and they marched through the streets like celebrities. Gabe smiled.

"What are you thinking about, nerd?" Wynnie asked. They poked Gabe in the shoulder. "Is it Relle? Because if it is, then I don't want to know."

"No," Gabe said. Not that he hadn't also thought of Relle forgiving him when he returned a hero to the island, having found a doctor, a hospital, medicine. He didn't know if he should worry about that. Was it okay to want to be a hero? "I'm thinking about the base."

"Me too," Wynnie said. "I miss school. Maybe they have a school. I know we kind of have school, and I was never really into middle school when the real thing was around, but I miss the stupid stuff like Spirit Week and snow days and worrying about tests. I never thought I would miss tests, but I do."

Gabe understood. "Remember complaining about the ferry?" he asked. His mother ranted about it. Constantly. It made traveling for games and really everything incredibly difficult. And when they missed it, they had to wait hours for the next one.

Wynnie laughed. "And now it takes us four days, if we're lucky, to make it a few hours by car. Man, the end of the world sucks."

The farther they got from Maine, the more congested the world seemed. There were cars everywhere. Tractor trailers. Minivans. Motorcycles. They were so tight together in spots, Gabe and Wynnie had to crawl on top of the vehicles.

The houses got closer together as more sprouted up like colorful weeds along the route. And then they spread back out and grew bigger and bigger.

"I want that one," Wynnie would say. "No, that one," to each mansion they passed. They were yellow or brown or white wood. They were simple and huge and expensive. Some were still perfect. Some had caved-in roofs or shattered windows from the big trees in the yards.

Then they were turning down a road that had office buildings with medical names. Soon the offices fell away, and a national park and old fences that Gabe could barely make out under the tall grass took their place. Gabe pulled up his binoculars.

A little way down, the road ran straight into a fence. A different fence from the split logs of the park. This fence was metal and menacing. It was as tall as the trees in the forest. Behind the closed gate was a small building, a guard station.

Gabe felt a flutter in his stomach. Of nerves and excitement and potential.

The base.

Gabe and Wynnie walked closer together than they had been. And in complete silence as they stepped up to the looming gate. A boy, not much older than Gabe, clean shaven and wearing a green camouflage uniform, came out of a guard station on the other side. A low growl rumbled in Mud's throat.

Across the guard's chest was a gun, a very large gun, that was not like the hunting rifle Peter had kept locked up on the island. Unease made sweat gather along Gabe's hairline. Wynnie blew out air next to him, and Gabe stepped closer to his friend.

"Who are you?" the soldier asked. "Where are you from?"

"Oh," Gabe said. *Get it together, Sweeney, the gun isn't pointed at you,* he reasoned to himself. *But it could be,* burrowed next to the thought. Gabe tried to relax. To loosen his rigid shoulders. To fake confidence. "Gabe Sweeney and Wynnie Hogan. We're . . . well, we survived. And we live on an island in Maine. We saw our first survivor about a month ago, and now we've just seen two more that came from here. They wanted our supplies. I guess . . . I guess we just wanted to know there were more people out there."

The boy regarded Gabe. He was maybe eighteen. Maybe younger. A nametag said Yellowhair. "You'll need to come back in the morning. The major will be here then. He'll want to talk to you." He rested his hand on the gun, and Gabe understood it meant the conversation was over.

Come back. It wasn't like they could stay at a hotel.

"I guess it's not a no," he mumbled to Wynnie. He was trying to stay positive, but he was hungry and tired. And he had built up the idea that they would have a bed to sleep in. And food. And the way things used to be.

There were houses on the road outside the gate and an Irish pub that smelled like mildew. It felt like there were ghosts whispering in the woods.

"This is creepy," Wynnie said. "Can we build a fire? I'm going to build a fire."

"You don't want to stay in the pub?"

"No," Wynnie said. "It smelled weird and it was too dark from all these trees."

Mud did not run into the woods and hunt. She stayed close while Gabe hung their hammocks and Wynnie made a fire with leaves and wood and the matches they had packed. It puffed smoke at first, then blazed warm. They were all good at building fires now. Gabe put a shirt down on the ground for his dog to sleep on.

"What do you think they're doing at home?" Wynnie asked. "Practicing for the talent show?"

Gabe pictured the house. The big living room. "Maybe. Or if they already had it, I bet Malachi's talking to Chloe or Violet. Maybe both of them." He smiled. "I bet Relle's playing Scrabble." She was probably going to destroy him when he got back.

Gabe realized, as he smiled, that he was homesick. That part of a vacation where you realized you wanted to go back to your bed. And this wasn't even close to a vacation, but that's how he felt.

He leaned back in his hammock and watched the flames drive away the ghosts.

The little island was home.

In the morning, Gabe woke up to a dead fire, Mud barking, and a boot kicking him in the foot. "Get up," a voice said. Gabe stumbled out of his hammock. Blurry-eyed, he watched Wynnie do the same.

It was a guard. A different teenage guard. And a man who Gabe assumed was the major.

"That's unnecessary, airman," he said. The man was about the age of Gabe's parents. Other than Sylvia and Peter, Gabe hadn't seen another parent-aged adult in two years. He immediately wondered how the major had survived, when his own parents hadn't. It made him angry.

Both the guard and the major were wearing medical masks over their faces.

"Where do you live?" the major asked. "Maine? With how many others? What are you eating? How are you getting fuel? Are you willing to trade for it?"

It was a lot to answer. Gabe glanced over at Wynnie. "How are you getting fuel?" he asked back. "We'd like to see the base."

"No," the major said. "Now tell me about your supplies. Are you preppers?"

"No," Gabe said. The major seemed very interested in what they had on the island and how they had gotten it. Almost desperate. With no mention of the men who Malachi had encountered. "We aren't preppers. I'll tell you about the island if you let us see the base."

"Gabe," Wynnie said.

Above the mask, the major's eyes regarded the boy. A lot like Sylvia did. His head foggy with sleep, his body aching, Gabe squared his shoulders. He had information the major wanted, and he was going to get something out of the deal.

"We're a group of twenty up in Maine," Wynnie explained. "We don't need supplies or anything. We just didn't know there were other people alive."

"We have about one hundred. We estimate, though we aren't sure, a few thousand left over the whole country."

A few thousand. Gabe's heart beat furiously. That was more than he'd thought. Thousands more. He wanted to cry. Where were they all? How had they survived? And how did the military know? Were they in contact with anyone?

That hope he felt when he first saw Relle throbbed in his chest.

"Fine. You'll need to be decontaminated," the major said. He turned and walked. "If you'll follow me."

Gabe and Wynnie followed behind, but Wynnie stopped. They yanked on Gabe's sleeve until he stopped. Mud stopped too. "I don't want to go," Wynnie whispered.

Gabe turned his head. "What do you mean, you don't want to go?"

"I mean I don't want to go."

"Wynnie." He wanted to say so many things. He wanted to roll his eyes. They were finally getting to see other people. Why did Wynnie want to leave now? "You told Sylvia you wanted to go to the base with me, and they're letting us on the base."

"Yeah, but I don't like it," Wynnie said. "I've got a bad feeling. Decontaminated?"

Gabe was frustrated. He was sore and tired and now that the major was letting them go into the base, why didn't Wynnie want to follow? He scratched his jaw. "I assume it's in case we're carrying the virus or any other diseases." He said it as politely as possible.

"If we had whatever killed the world, we'd be dead too," Wynnie said.

Gabe knew they were right, but he didn't know how to respond.

"Is everything okay?" the major asked. Kim, his nametag read. That was his last name.

"Yes," Gabe said.

And Wynnie said, "No."

"Okay!" Gabe said. He was yelling and whispering, but Kim was listening anyway. "Okay." That time was calmer. There was no way he wasn't going in after coming this far. "Then you and Mud stay here, and I will go."

"No, I don't want to be alone," Wynnie said. "I'm coming with you."

Gabe shook his head. *Get it together, Sweeney. Stop shaking your head.* So he smiled at the major. "Ready when you are, Major."

18

Gabe was definitely frustrated as they walked to the gate and then stepped through the door. He was frustrated when they stood in front of a white trailer with CAUTION and DIRTY written in bold black letters on it.

"There are three rooms," the major said. "A dirty room where you will remove your infected clothing, a shower facility, and a clean room where you will dress in the scrubs in the lockers. You can get your clothing back when you leave the base."

Wynnie went first, and Gabe waited. He looked around. The road they had followed to get to the base continued on down a small hill. To the left and right were more roads. The trees and lawns were much more manicured than outside the gate, but less manicured than the old world. It was shaggy, like maybe the landscapers would show up tomorrow. But he assumed this was just how it looked now.

When it was his turn, he left Mud and climbed three metal steps. The dirty side was cold. He took his clothes off and placed them in a bag on the bench. Gabe opened the sealed door with the metal handle. In the second room, he showered and didn't look too hard at himself in the big mirrors on both sides. He was skinnier than he wanted to be. Maybe they had burgers on the base. His stomach growled.

In the third room, he opened the lockers until he found a top and bottom labeled MEDIUM. Blue scrubs like a surgeon. Gabe hooked the surgical mask around his ears and felt sick. His hands shook. His father had worn blue scrubs sometimes.

Gabe's eyes burned and he took a deep breath. Wiped his wet eyes. *Okay*, he said to himself, *that's enough.*

He stepped outside in the slippers provided and immediately patted Mud on the head. Ran his hand over her ear. He was okay. He was ready.

Wynnie was wearing green scrubs. They were too big on them. Gabe was glad, so immensely grateful, that Wynnie had come. That he had a friend with him.

"This way," the major said. He gestured toward a four-wheeled vehicle that looked a little like a golf cart. But bigger and heavy duty and green.

Gabe frowned. Peter would have thought using fuel was a bad idea. They were going to run out of it soon, but Gabe kept his thoughts to himself. The guard drove, and the major sat next to him.

"Are you a pilot?" Wynnie asked, when they passed the hangars.

"No." That's all the major said. It wasn't very friendly. Gabe glanced at Wynnie, who shrugged.

The guard drove past a building that the major said were the dorms. Then a white satellite and parking lots. A graveyard. It looked like the old one on the big island from Before. Gabe looked away quickly and rested his hand on Mud's head. He cleared his throat.

They turned left at a monument of an old military airplane. It was yellow and brown, and hovering in the air. The guard stopped at what Gabe guessed was a school with big windows and a basketball court out front. It looked so normal, it relaxed Gabe. He dropped his hands into his lap.

"This is our school," the major said. "Would you like to see?"

"Yeah, okay," Gabe said.

They got out of the vehicle. Mud smelled a tree, and Gabe told her to stay close. The four of them followed the circular sidewalk leading to the entrance and opened the glass doors. Gabe realized, looking at the school, he would have been finishing eighth grade. It would be lacrosse season. He thought about time this way a lot. Oh, this is when we would be having winter break. This would have been a snow day. Today would be state testing. The eighth-grade formal dance at the end of the year where everyone wore dresses and tuxedoes. That sort of thing. He measured his time by the school year. He wondered when that would slip away, and he would measure time in some other way.

This school didn't look like Gabe's. It looked close to brand-new and bright. Gabe's was supposed to get a renovation the summer the world ended, which never happened. The entryway to this one led to a big room. A cafeteria. There were stairs and a stage too, one he imagined Relle would love for the talent show. Everything was modern and warm. Brightly lit. They had electricity.

"You have electricity?" Gabe said.

"Generators," the major said.

Generators ran on gas. *Where were they getting gas? Maybe*

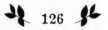

it was solar. Gabe wasn't sure. Maybe it was jet fuel. Peter said that lasted a little longer than regular gas.

"And the kids?" Wynnie asked.

Kim looked at his watch. "They should be here shortly."

And then, like he had commanded it, a line of children streamed into the cafeteria, followed by a teacher. The group looked to be under ten or so, like Bear and Delphine and Mason. They were wiggly and trying not to reach out their hands to each other. A few of them were successful.

"Wow," Wynnie whispered. "I haven't seen this many kids in a long time."

More walked in. So many kids, four or five times what they had on the island, from elementary to high school. It was so strange. They lined up for lunch and went to seats with trays full of food like everything was normal. Like the world had never ended. Gabe was sad and overwhelmed by all of them. He was used to the same twenty faces of the little island.

The smell of vegetables and meat and people filled the cafeteria. He had forgotten what lunchtime smelled like. *Was this it? Had they found normal?*

"Can we eat?" Gabe asked.

Kim sighed. "One meal. And then you tell me about where you came from."

Gabe and Wynnie lined up with a class of teens. "This is weird," Wynnie whispered. "Not bad weird, just weird." Everyone was staring in their direction. The little kids would look and giggle. Talk to the kid in the seat next to them. The older kids looked without speaking.

"Yeah," Gabe agreed. He pulled a blue tray from the stack. It was damp like it had just been washed. He couldn't believe so many people had outlasted the end of the world.

"How'd y'all survive?" The boy ahead of him in line turned around. His voice was Southern, not like he was from Boston. He had shiny black hair that skimmed his eyes and wore clothes like he skateboarded.

Gabe shook his head. "We don't really know. We were on a small island offshore in Maine."

"Cool," the boy said. He nodded. "I'm from North Carolina. They shipped me to a base down there first, right when everything happened, with a few other kids, and then when we ran out of food last year, our oldest farm kid drove us up here."

"How'd you run out of food?" Wynnie asked. "Didn't the adults scavenge or anything?"

"We had one adult down there," the boy said. "And then he got bit by a snake and died."

"I'm sorry," Gabe said.

The boy scooped potato puffs in the shape of smiles onto his tray, and Gabe did the same. He hadn't seen them in years. Farther down, he got a burger with a square of plasticky cheese in between a bun. He felt like he was in a different dimension. Like it was a different Gabe scooping cafeteria food, and the real him was on the island. "Where did you get this food?"

"I don't know," the boy said. "I heard kids saying we're running out, though."

"Don't you plant a garden or anything?" Wynnie asked. "Or search restaurants for staples?"

"We mostly use frozen vegetables," he said. "A few of us go hunting for deer after school like Before. Make jerky out of it." He picked up a plastic fork. "I'm Sam, by the way."

Gabe and Wynnie introduced themselves. They followed the boy to a table and sat. Sam bit into a smiley face.

Like he was a reflection in a mirror, Gabe did the same. The potato puff tasted like a freezer. It was bland compared to the fresh potatoes they had grown and Sylvia had taught them to cook with seasoning and oil.

"Do you see many new people?" Wynnie asked.

"Ah, sometimes we get new kids," Sam said. "We let them stay if they want."

"We saw two men from here, well, someone on our island did. Two men who were kicked out?" Gabe asked. He couldn't imagine kicking out Sylvia or Peter. They knew so much more than the rest of them.

"Ah, no teeth? I know them," Sam said. "They were hoarding supplies. Crashed a car into the major's house. Weren't helping. They were *adults*, ya know? And they never did anything useful." He bit his hamburger. "So you're staying with us now?"

"No," Gabe blurted. "No, we're just here to . . ." He scowled and looked at Major Kim. The man was leaning against a wall, watching them. The longer they were at the base, the more frustrated Gabe felt. Where was the doctor? What was their plan when the gas ran out? When there were no longer frozen vegetables for the lunch line. Peter and Sylvia would never let that happen. They had taught the kids on the island how to be resourceful. How to can fruits and vegetables for the long winter. How to keep the flies away from the animals. Gabe realized, along with the history lessons in the mornings, he knew so much more than he did when he left the big island.

"We didn't know there were other survivors," Wynnie said.

"Well, when you get home, we'll have to talk over ham radio. Do y'all have a ham radio?" Sam asked.

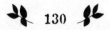

"What's a ham radio?" Wynnie asked.

"It's the end of the world and y'all don't know what a ham radio is?" Sam shoved the rest of his burger into his mouth and wiped his hands on his shorts. "Finish your lunch!"

Gabe picked up his cheeseburger. It looked like one from elementary school. He remembered kids getting them, but he mostly brought a sandwich in a lunchbox. He bit and chewed. It was warm. It tasted gray. It did not taste like the cheeseburgers of his daydreams. He wondered what they were eating for lunch on the little island.

He wondered what they were doing at home. He imagined Bear would be giggling and running around. Lucas would be playing his guitar. Relle would be picking dandelions and reciting poetry from memory.

Gabe sighed. He wanted to see them. *What was wrong with him? He'd wanted to find the base so badly, and now that he'd found it, he wanted to go back?* It was embarrassing.

"Ready?" Sam stood up. "We're gonna get you a ham radio."

When Sam marched up to the major and pointed back at Gabe and Wynnie, they didn't know what to expect, but then they were all riding in the green golf cart with Mud—who had wandered onto the basketball courts and was getting petted by some older girls—to a building on the other side of base.

"Okay, now you need to tell me about your island," Kim said.

While they rode, Wynnie told Kim and Sam about their island. About their solar panels and how they conserved water and the foods they planted and scavenged. And Gabe was silent in the back. The base was supposed to have answers. The base was supposed to be normal. And while it was, it was too normal. Gabe felt like he and Wynnie knew more about surviving the end of the world than they did.

The day was getting warm. His hair was damp with sweat. The antiseptic smell of the decontamination trailer soap was strong on his skin.

"Hmm," Major Kim said, "we will have to incorporate some of those methods. Who taught you all this?"

Wynnie gushed about Sylvia and Peter.

They turned near the hangars and stopped at a low beige brick building. Kim took off his cap, and Gabe and Wynnie and Mud followed him through the doors. Inside, it was cool and the lighting dim. A few teens in the same green uniforms as Kim walked around the room like it was a regular office building. The airmen, Gabe figured. Pictures of airmen of the quarter were in neat frames on the wall. The old president was at the top. Gabe wondered if he was still in charge.

Major Kim pulled one of them aside and the boy came back with a small black radio with a curly cord connecting two pieces.

"Have you ever used one of these before?" the airman asked Gabe and Wynnie. He was young and seemed annoyed. Little red pimples lined his cheeks.

"No," they both said and shook their heads.

The airman showed them how to turn it on, how to type in the frequencies, which were like stations on a radio, and how to call out. He had them practice in front of him. He scolded Wynnie when they typed in the wrong number.

He wrote down something on a scrap of paper. "You'll need to get a book, like a user manual, from a bookstore or library. I don't have one here. We mostly listen, but we do a broadcast on Sundays at 1800 at this frequency."

"That's six at night," Sam said. "And you can call me whenever you want. I mean, unless I'm in school. It's like a phone number." He added his call number, a mix of numbers and letters, to the paper, and Gabe held it in his fist.

"You used to have to have a license, but not during emergencies," the major said. He was much nicer now that they told him about the island. He almost smiled. "I'd say this counts as one."

"Thanks," Wynnie said. "That's cool. We haven't talked to anyone since . . . wow. It's like having a phone again, kind of."

In the golf cart, the major and Sam brought them to the gate, where, a few hours before, they had started the day much differently. Gabe hopped off the back seat and Mud did the same, spinning in a circle near the guard building.

"You can go get your stuff back from decontamination," the major said.

"We'll talk soon!" Sam said. "I haven't left the base since we got here, but maybe I'll come visit you."

"Yeah, of course," Gabe said. "We'll talk to you when we figure out how to work the radio."

"The pork radio," Wynnie said. "The bacon radio."

For the first time in two years, they'd be able to contact the rest of the world. Whatever that was.

They changed in the decontamination trailers and grabbed their packs. Gabe carefully folded his father's sweater. He and Wynnie started the first leg of the trip home, and they didn't speak except for an occasional "I have to pee," or "That burger was gross, right?"

The farther they got from base, the more annoyed Gabe felt. It was like asking for a video game system for Christmas and getting a pair of socks. Gabe had wanted to find a doctor or to eat a cheeseburger that was actually good or to know that the world was intact somewhere. And instead they had found people still acting like it was Before. It wasn't Before anymore. Survivors needed to adapt and change to the new world—didn't they realize that? The more they walked, the angrier Gabe felt, until there was a great big hole in the middle of his chest.

Gabe wasn't supposed to have the answers. The base was supposed to. He was frustrated. Frustrated that he had expected some kind of answer. Frustrated that there wasn't. And frustrated that he had hoped.

What was the point of hope? Gabe would never start high school. He would never have a spring pep rally for lacrosse. He wouldn't go to the prom or have a graduation or go to college. He wouldn't get married. Who got married at the end of the world? And if he did, his parents wouldn't be there.

Gabe's dad always said it was okay to be sad. It was even fine to wallow, but eventually you had to pull yourself out. He decided he would let himself wallow until they stopped for the night.

To help, he played a little game to change his mood. If Malachi were with them, he'd be running through the grass pretending to be a deer or a Revolutionary soldier or really anything. And it would spread joy. It

would pour over all of them. Or Relle. Relle would come up with some idea to cheer everyone up. Some game or activity that Gabe could never dream of. She looked forward to things. She made other people look forward to things.

It wasn't working. Nothing was working. Each step brought him no closer to peace.

"What are you thinking about?" Wynnie asked.

He grunted for an answer because he had too many thoughts, and then felt bad, so he asked, "What are you thinking about?"

Mud ran into the pines at the intersection where they needed to turn. Gabe whistled so she knew where they were.

"I'm thinking," Wynnie said, "that it was nice to see other people, but I like the island more." Their voice was happy and light. "Thinking how lucky I am to go back to a house, my house where my family is."

It was a very grateful thought that slightly rubbed off on Gabe. Yes, he was thankful for Sylvia and Peter. They had helped him survive.

They walked all day, and the sun was warm on their backs. In Andover, Gabe and Wynnie stopped. They followed the signs for the prep school and stood in front of the wide, overgrown lawn. "Should we stay here

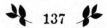 137

tonight?" Gabe asked. He was tired. The buildings were big and brick and beautiful. No outward damage that he could see.

It was a big campus. There was a chapel, an archaeology museum, dorms, libraries. Gabe made the mistake of walking into the gym. There was no sign near the front door, and it didn't look like a gym. It was the same brick as the library. But it was full of bodies. Gabe held his breath and shut the door quietly. He trembled outside it and felt sick to his stomach.

"What was it?" Wynnie asked.

"A gym. They'd made a hospital."

"Ah Gabe, I'm sorry. Let's go back to the library. There are couches we can sleep on."

They ate granola bars in the library. There were big couches that were covered in soft blue velvet. Gabe stretched out on his back. It was much more comfortable than the hammock of the night before. The ceiling was painted with light blues and yellows. Stars and clouds and moons.

He looked at his watch. At home, it was time for dinner. He wondered who was cooking and what they were eating. He imagined walking through the front door. He hoped they would be happy with the radio.

Gabe flipped to his side. He was done wallowing. "I'm happy to go home to the island too," he said. Wynnie was looking through yearbooks. They had a stack of them near their knee, and they were leaning against the wall, their face in the pages.

"Cool," they said. "Me too."

"What do you want to do?"

"This." Wynnie nodded to the yearbooks. "These are some rich kids. I kind of hate them all." Wynnie pretended to vomit.

Gabe stood up. Maybe there were medical books, different ones from the library at home. He found the nonfiction section and ran his fingers along the spines, reading the titles. Biology textbooks, which he read on the island and didn't much enjoy because they were dry. Books about the future of medicine, which made him half laugh. That future hadn't exactly happened. He found one, though, about antibiotics and how to make your own.

The man who'd invented antibiotics, bacteria killers, changed the world because his lab was dirty. Mold had grown on a contaminated staph plate, and the scientist realized the staph bacteria had been killed by the mold. Before that, ancient cultures had used moldy bread on wounds.

A thrill ran up Gabe's spine and his mind started to race. Maybe they could make their own antibiotics. If they were careful. He'd have to check with Sylvia first. He sat on the big couch and thought about how they'd make mold. It would have to be clean, disinfected. Boiled. And then grown on glass.

The possibility made him excited, like when he'd found Relle in the woods and first heard her talk. Like when he'd found out there were survivors at the base.

It spurred him into action. Gabe went to the aisle with books on electronics and found a ham radio manual, a simple one with a yellow cover, and read twenty pages before he fell asleep.

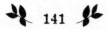

Gabe slept heavy and dreamed about uniforms and Morse code and clouds that sprouted into mold. It wasn't a bad dream. But he woke up drooling and groggy, Mud licking his hand. Gabe groaned and stood up after a minute. He let the dog outside and thought about what they would tell the others when they got back.

Gabe replayed the words from Major Kim and Sam. There were potentially thousands of people in what used to be the United States. The rest of the island would like to know that. He imagined telling Relle.

They were eager to get home and walked farther that day than they had traveling to the base. It was dusk, the sky the purple of almost summer, when they realized they needed to stop and find a spot for the night. But they hadn't seen a building or house in a long time, Gabe noticed. It was all green plants and gray road.

"Wynnie, we need to find somewhere to camp."

"Not here, we don't," Wynnie whispered.

Mud growled low, deep in her throat, and stood stock-still, her leg pointed into the darkness. Gabe squinted. "What is it?" He made his voice soft like Wynnie's, even though the hairs on his neck made him want to shout.

"Pigs."

The pigs on the island were fat and grazed a lot in the summer. But the older kids had to teach the younger ones not to pet them. Farm pigs would bite fingers. Even eat fingers.

Gabe didn't know what feral pigs would eat.

Twenty yards away from Gabe and Wynnie, in a thick tangle of overgrown bushes, was a group of them. Maybe twenty pigs. They were thinner than the island pigs. And taller.

And they were staring at the two kids and dog.

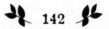

"They can't see well," Gabe whispered. But he knew they could smell just as well as Mud, and his stomach flipped over at the thought.

Mud brought her head down. Her hair went up on her back.

"Mud," Gabe whispered. "You stay here."

She was six feet from Gabe. Not far at all. But too far if she bolted. Gabe's fingers shook. He was very aware of the devastation he would feel, and started to feel already, if Mud bolted toward a pack of wild pigs.

Gabe took a quiet step toward Mud. He hoped she was too distracted to hear him. He took another step. And another.

And Gabe lunged at his dog.

21

Gabe had gotten Mud when she was one, for his birthday present when he turned eight.

Mud was from the pound and had no manners. She bit. She chewed on everything. She wasn't potty-trained. Gabe's mom was good with dogs. Patient. "We just need to teach her. She'll be well-behaved before you know it." And it was true. Just like that, she was a good dog.

Gabe couldn't lose her. She was all he had left.

He cursed. Her leash was in his pack. His fingers fumbled against her collar. But he tried a second time and wedged them under the red nylon. Gabe held tight. "Let's go, Muddy," he whispered.

Gabe didn't look at the pigs, but he felt their eyes on his back as he and Wynnie walked away as fast as they could, their backpacks heavy.

It wasn't until they were safely away that he let the dog go. And then he lectured her. "Don't do that again." Though she hadn't done anything wrong. "You stay close." Though he knew he would let her hunt and wander soon. "I don't want to lose you."

The dog looked up at him. He smiled at her eyebrows. He loved that she had eyebrows.

"Just don't do anything stupid," he said. Like that was the compromise.

Mud trotted ahead of him.

"Uggghhhh," he groaned at Wynnie.

"I'm ready to be home," they said.

"Yeah. Me too."

The sky was black, so they made a camp on the road, which was terrible. And Gabe tossed and turned on the hard ground at first, Mud curled up between the kids. He dreamed of pigs and soft beds and Scrabble.

In the morning, they walked, stiff. They played a guessing game of people and places and things with twenty questions. Gabe lost. He had forgotten the name of a movie, but he could picture the last scene in his head. It annoyed him when that happened. There was nowhere to look it up.

By afternoon, the sun was hot. Gabe took his shirt off and wrapped it around his head. His stomach was very white, and they did not have sunscreen. He would have to put his shirt back on soon.

"You look stupid," Wynnie said.

"I don't care." He stepped around a car. It felt nice to feel the sun. But if he were with someone else, Relle perhaps, he wouldn't have done it. He wasn't sure. Maybe he would. Probably soon they'd all go swimming again, if Sylvia wasn't worried about the men from the base still. Relle said she was a good swimmer. Maybe they'd race to the rocks. He'd like to do that.

He thought about what she looked like in a swimsuit.

Gabe cleared his throat. "Can we go look in there?" He pointed at a gray-and-blue Walmart, the *t* falling off. "I need sunscreen." Like gas, the sunscreen would go bad soon. He figured Sylvia had a plan for that.

The parking lot was scattered with cars. There was no rhyme or reason. Some in the front. Some in the back.

Some parked carefully between lines. And others askew. The doors to the store had been barricaded on one side, but the other was busted open.

Inside was dark. Gabe heard animals. What kind, he wasn't sure, and it sent a chill up him, remembering the pigs. It was probably mice or rats, he knew. That did not comfort him. "You stay with me, Mud."

He used his flashlight and Wynnie used theirs, and they headed toward the clothes.

The pharmacy was a mess, but Gabe still looked through it. He got some prednisone, a steroid, because Mason was asthmatic, and inhalers for the same reason. He got antibiotics, even though they were expired, because they still helped with infections. An EpiPen too. In the sunscreen aisle, he sprayed his chest and back. He worried Relle would think he was too skinny and scowled.

"Wynnie!" he yelled. He didn't know where they were. Gabe walked back through the pharmacy section. To his right, he shone his flashlight at the seasonal area. It was Fourth of July and cookout themed. There were sparklers and red, white, and blue beads. Grill accessories and Stars and Stripes bowls and serving dishes.

He called his friend's name again and kept walking. Past the women's clothing. Tank tops with flags and puns. To his left were the checkout lanes.

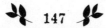

"Wynnie!"

Gabe was at the doors they'd come in. Near the grocery half. A few bags of bread remained, moldy in their plastic. He thought about bringing one home but decided against it. Carrying moldy bread for days sounded gross.

Gabe turned around.

Standing in front of him was a woman, with a baby strapped to her chest.

She was holding a gun.

And it was pointed at him.

Gabe had prayed a lot when he didn't hear from his family. He had prayed that they would call him on the cell phone that stayed silent. That the whole nightmare would be over. And when that never happened, he stopped praying. He was not praying now, a gun pointed at his chest.

He *was* willing his dog to come to him. Or Wynnie. *Where was Wynnie?*

He whistled loud for Mud. *Why wasn't that dog better behaved?*

Gabe thought he could wrestle the gun away from the woman if he needed to. She was smaller than him and had a baby hooked to her. But also, she had *a baby* hooked to her. He did not want to hurt the baby. Or her.

He was hoping he could talk her down from pointing the gun at him. He was good at talking. Except with Relle. He thought about Relle and how he liked her hair and how weird she was. He wished he had been kinder to her. She deserved kindness. Selfishly, he wished, if he were going to die right now, that he had kissed her and not Violet. But he was thankful he had written Relle the note.

That was brave of him. He was proud of that.

But he had told little Bear he wouldn't die, and so he needed to keep his promise.

"My name is Gabe Sweeney," he said. "And I am fourteen years old. I just needed sunscreen." He raised his hands up to his ears. "I won't hurt you."

"Of course you won't hurt me," she said. "I'm the one with the gun."

She was small with long brown hair and light brown skin. The baby blinked bright brown eyes at him.

Gabe marveled that this baby had been born in the After. *Wasn't that impossible?* That the mother had survived. That an infant had been created and survived birth. He hadn't seen a baby in years.

"You live here?" he asked. "I live on a farm. On an island in Maine. My friend and I left to see if there were more survivors in Massachusetts."

The woman's eyes filled with tears. "Were there?" she asked. "And you have someone with you?"

Gabe nodded. He took a step away from her. "I do." He kept his voice soft. But he wanted to run. If Wynnie were with him, he would. He didn't want to separate from them.

Mud came bounding toward Gabe, and when she saw the woman, she tiptoed over and wiggled her butt while she smelled the woman's foot. The baby watched the dog and gurgled.

"That's Mud," he said. "We won't hurt you, honest. I was looking for supplies, and we are headed back to Maine. We saw people in Massachusetts, and they gave us a radio so we can contact them and others. You could go find them. We could tell you how to get there. Or you could come with us. Our island is a family."

Malachi. Sylvia. Bear. *Relle.* Sometimes you found family. Like a lost pen. He moved his feet so slightly, it barely felt like he had budged. "Are *you* alone?" He asked because of the baby and because he didn't know if he should run. Gabe regretted not having a separation plan with Wynnie. Where *were* they?

"Maybe," she said. "Maybe there are a hundred people behind me."

"Maybe," he said. He took another small, so small, step back. He wanted to scream for Wynnie so they could leave.

"We have electricity," he told the woman. "We have water. We have anything you could need."

"Then why did you leave?" she asked.

And Gabe didn't quite know the answer to that. Not then. Not with a gun pointed at him.

"Gabe, I found Doritos. Cool Ranch!" he heard. "Like five bags. This is the best day. Forget the pigs last night. Doritos!"

Wynnie. Walking toward him, their head buried in bags of chips.

"Don't move," the woman said. She and Gabe were both staring at Wynnie, who stopped and dropped the blue bags.

"Oh, you've got to be kidding me," Wynnie said. "I take it back. Worst day." They put their hands up like Gabe. "You needed that sunscreen, didn't you? *I'm Gabe Sweeney, and skincare is really important to me.*"

The sunscreen. "See?" Gabe asked the woman. Gently. "I just wanted sunscreen. We'll leave. We'll even leave the Doritos."

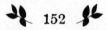

Wynnie groaned. "Gabe, if we're going to die right now, I should probably tell you that Relle definitely likes you. I heard her talking to her imaginary friend about it."

Gabe stared at Wynnie. *What?* Relle *liked* him? If the situation were different, he would have hugged Wynnie. Or whooped. Or jumped in the air like Malachi. But he couldn't. There was a gun pointed at him.

"We have almost died multiple times, Wynnie! You couldn't tell me then?"

"It never came up," they said, shrugging.

"I'm not going to kill you." The gun barrel, the one that stared him down, started to lower.

Gabe let out a huge sigh, but kept his hands raised.

"I'm Prerna," she said. "Take us with you."

Wynnie yanked on Gabe's elbow, and they stood with their backs to the woman and the baby. "Can we just invite people to the island?" they whispered. "What will Sylvia say?"

"She's got a baby," Gabe said. They were standing out of earshot. He peeked behind him. Prerna was watching them closely, the gun, thankfully, still lowered. "Sylvia took Relle in because she was a kid."

"I'm just saying," Wynnie said. "We could tell her about the base."

"I *did* tell her," Gabe said. "She wants to come to the island."

"Fine," Wynnie said. "Fine, you're right. I just . . . the gun and everything. And I dropped my Doritos."

"You can have the Doritos," Prerna said.

Maybe they weren't out of earshot.

They slept on mattresses that night, in the back part of the store that used to be the employee break room. Prerna had turned it into her home. There were candles and posters and a couch. A crib for the baby, Parth, though he slept with his mother in her bed.

Mud was a traitor and slept with the newcomer too. She had done it with Relle also. *Relle.* Wynnie's announcement changed everything. Gabe could think of nothing else. It was even worse than before.

In the morning, Prerna gave them a breakfast of rice and beans cooked on a little propane grill. And then they packed and were off. Prerna said goodbye to her make-shift home.

They walked for two more days. Wynnie told jokes. Gabe daydreamed about the girl with red hair. Prerna told them about moving to the United States from India when she was six. The dog trotted. And Parth slept and cried and was fed. They covered fifty miles until they were close to home.

When they hit the town with the McDonald's and the marina with the broken lighthouse, Gabe felt immense relief and joy. He pulled out the rowboat that was hidden in the bushes and tried to remember putting it there. It felt like years ago. It had been nine days. Nine days and now they stared at the island like it was a mirage.

Gabe rowed. The boat was full. Maybe too full, but they did it anyway. The shore in sight, Gabe turned to see the kids storm the beach. The little ones waded in, shouting across the water at them. Gabe felt like weeping. He didn't want to weep, but to see home was . . . well, it was overwhelming, and Gabe wondered why he'd wanted to leave in the first place.

When they reached the shore, Mud jumped out and chased Bear, and they splashed around each other. Wynnie helped Prerna out of the boat. The kids crowded around her and the baby. Gabe looked for Relle

immediately. Even before he stopped rowing, he was searching. Her cheeks were pink and bright. She looked even happier than when she'd first arrived on the island. She was wearing a summer dress. Light blue and floaty. He cleared his throat.

Violet squealed. "A baby!"

Parth was a huge hit. And Prerna looked happy and overwhelmed, which Gabe understood. He had felt the same way at the base. Prerna hadn't seen many people in the last two years, and Gabe and Wynnie hadn't asked too much about it.

The group walked through the Avenue, and Gabe remembered bringing Relle through it the first time. The flowers were gone now. Gabe looked at Relle again. *She liked him. Relle Douglas liked him.* He didn't know how to act. Then he scowled because Wynnie was right. The only thing, the only person, who made him nervous was Relle.

"How was it?" Malachi asked. "Find the base?"

Gabe nodded, distracted. How was he going to talk to her, alone? He probably should let her come to him, shouldn't he? Since he wrote the note. It was her turn. If he went to her, it would be too pushy. He didn't want to be a pushy guy. They were terrible.

He groaned. He wished he had someone to ask about this.

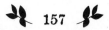

"What—not good? Did you eat a burger? See a zombie? Discover aliens exist?" Malachi clapped him on the shoulder.

He had to focus. "No zombies, but there are people. Lots of them. They think thousands."

"Man, thousands? For real?" Malachi pointed at his mouth. "Did you see those guys again? No teeth. My nemesises. Nemeses? My nemeses!"

Gabe shook his head. "No, but we did get a radio so we can call the base. So we can call other people. What about here? Anything new?"

"I'm taking over Peter's garden duty," Malachi said. "Call me Farmer Mac, the prettiest farmer on the east coast. The greenest thumb around, baby!"

The kids rushed to the house, and the familiarity of it slammed into Gabe. Sylvia met them and hugged him and Wynnie hard. "You're back," she said. "You were good?" And she let go just as quickly. She gushed over the baby, squeezing his toes and asking if he needed a sweater.

"This is Prerna," Wynnie said. "And Parth!"

They all sat around the table, like they had when Relle had arrived, and Gabe and Wynnie, and then Prerna, took turns telling the little island about the trip. About the people on the base and the pigs and the radio.

Gabe pulled it out of his pack. "I have to read about it more, but we can call. It's not just us anymore."

He realized he was proud of that, that they had come back with something useful. Whatever he had gone to the base for hadn't happened. Life would never be normal again, but that didn't mean that it would be bad. Wasn't a baby proof of that? That there was a future?

"What did we miss?" he asked. And he meant it. He wanted to know that Mason had burned the eggs and Malachi had gone clamming and that Sylvia was maybe going to let them go to the beach since they hadn't seen the two men from the base in so long.

"We postponed the talent show," Relle said. She stuck her chin out, and Gabe had to be very careful not to stare at her like he thought she had the most beautiful chin in the world. "So Wynnie wouldn't miss it."

"Yes!" Wynnie said. "I was hoping you would!"

"What about Gabe?" Bear asked. "Will he be in the talent show? What will you do?"

"Oh," Gabe said. Everyone looked at him, and he squirmed inside. He thought the talent show would have happened while he and Wynnie were gone, and while it didn't make him angry anymore, he still didn't want to participate. *Wasn't that for the little kids? And didn't he have other things to do?* He needed to get the ham radio set up and ask Sylvia about growing the antibiotics. Those were more important anyway. "I can't wait to see your play, Bear."

"Why do you have to be such a mushroom?" Malachi asked.

Gabe was tired. Very tired. He went upstairs to his room early while the others spent the evening in the living room playing games and passing around the baby.

It wasn't dark yet, and Gabe put his things away and his dirty clothes in the laundry. He was gentle with his father's sweater and took a shower and changed. The shower was nice. It was just as good as before. And it was much better than a pond or decontamination trailer.

Gabe sat on his bed and folded his hand across his chest. Tomorrow, he would read the rest of the manual and try calling Sam. He had written the base frequency in the yellow book and recorded Sam's again as well. He was excited.

His bed felt so nice too. It smelled like home. And propped behind his head, his pillows were just the right thickness. Gabe stared at the white closet doors and listened to the sounds of the island downstairs. He felt content.

A figure appeared in the doorway of his bedroom.

Relle.

Gabe shot straight up, then forced himself to fake ease. He sat on his bed again. It was gray and neat because Sylvia asked them to please make their bed every morning. Gabe didn't mind doing it—it made him feel productive, and he was thankful it was clean because the girl he liked was in his room. The girl *he liked.*

He wasn't entirely sure that was allowed. It wasn't something Sylvia had talked to them about, but it felt like a rule from the old world.

Why was Relle here? In his bedroom. Had she forgiven him? Did she like him still? Were they . . . well, were they going to kiss? She liked Gabe, right? That's what Wynnie had said. But now, back home, with Relle right in front of him, he wasn't quite so confident that was true. Maybe Wynnie had been teasing him. Maybe

Wynnie had just been trying to make the end of his life, a gun pointed at him, a little gentler.

Relax.

"Gabe," Relle said. And he wondered again about the power of the name thing she had mentioned.

"Uh-huh."

She stepped inside the room, and Gabe's heart did a strange, rolling thing in his chest. He sat up very straight and then immediately forced his body to loosen in the shoulders.

"I was in the barn, brushing one of the goats. Have you seen our newest, Clover? She has the most expressive eyes! I was talking to her because the barn is awfully quiet now without Peter." She stood at the end of his bed. "I suppose he never did talk very much, and I was the one always talking when I was out there with him." She laughed a little. And Gabe realized that he was definitely in love with her. And how terrible was it to be in love with someone if they weren't in love with you? Very, very terrible. "And I have a rash on my arm." She held it out for him to see. A line of red welts, which weren't freckles, ran up her forearm.

He took her wrist and felt his whole face burn. He cleared his throat. "I think it's probably just allergies. A little Benadryl will fix it, I bet."

Gabe awkwardly stood up and tried not to run to the bathroom for the medicine. Once he got there, he stared at himself in the mirror. "Relax, Sweeney. So embarrassing. This is how you act?" He shook his head to clear the love thoughts away. Relle wasn't there to kiss him. Which was disappointing. But she was there to ask for help. That was some consolation. And maybe she was using it as an excuse, because couldn't she have just used the Benadryl herself? She didn't really need Gabe's help, did she?

Not knowing how she felt was terrible. It was excruciating.

The sky was purple when he came back. It made pretty shadows on the walls. Gabe unscrewed the lid and squeezed a bit onto his finger. "Can I?" he asked. He was very quiet. He felt like there was a spell in the room. He kind of always felt that way when he was with Relle.

Relle nodded and held out her arm. Gabe took it, his heart wild. *Don't be embarrassing,* he told himself. He wiped it on her skin. "You could take the pill version instead," he said, "if it doesn't work. Or maybe a daily allergy pill before you go out to the barn. There's some in the bathroom. And wash your skin where you touch the goats when you're done."

"Thank you, Gabe."

Hearing his name made him feel bold. "Relle. Did you get my letter? Did you read it?"

The words flew out of him, and he wished immediately that he hadn't been so impulsive, so reckless. *What are you doing, Sweeney? You said you were going to let her come to you!*

Which she had, he reasoned.

But Relle pushed her chin out, which Gabe found very endearing. It usually meant she was going to say something very Relle-like.

"I did." It was short and not at all Relle-like.

"And?" he asked. And as he asked, he was kicking himself. *Please be quiet. What are you doing? This is not the plan.*

Relle went very still, which Gabe did not think was a good sign. He took a step back. Her arm dropped.

"You don't think I'm ridiculous? You didn't say you didn't think I was ridiculous." She furrowed her eyebrows, which he noticed, were red. "You said, 'I'm sorry for what happened,' which isn't the same as thinking I'm not ridiculous."

She said *ridiculous* so many times, he was dizzy. "I don't think you're ridiculous," he managed. "Not at all. I'm really sorry." Probably being honest, being sincere, was the best. He shook his head. "I don't know. I was

kind of . . . well, I was stuck. And sometimes I feel guilty for being happy. Because of . . . everything." He tried not to squeeze the little white tube in his hand. "I think I felt guilty about you. Because. You know. I liked. I *like*. You."

Why was it so hard to say? Saying it in the letter was so much easier.

It was dark now, in the shadows, which made it less terrible. Maybe she could barely see him, his discomfort.

"Hmm. I don't feel guilty for being happy," the red-haired girl said. "I like to think that the people we loved, the people we knew, and the people we never got to meet, are in the beautiful world around us. In the sea foam and the stretch of a tree branch. They can feel us. They can see us."

"I like that," Gabe told her.

"But," she said, "I have felt guilty for being sad. How can I be sad when I lived? When I have all these things in my life to be grateful for. I have a house and food—bread! I can take showers. I have friends and people who care about me. To feel sad, when I have all this, seems wrong. So I suppose we are opposites."

How could she think that—that it was wrong to be sad? That made no sense to him. It was a perfectly good time to be sad.

"It's okay to be sad," Gabe blurted out.

"It is. I *know* it is. I just don't always feel like I'm allowed to." Relle smiled. "And Gabe, you know, it's okay to be happy."

He was getting there.

25

The next day, Gabe whistled through chores. He floated during lessons—they had moved onto the 20th Maine and the Battle of Gettysburg. At lunch, he smiled at Relle across the table, and Malachi put him in a head-lock and called him goofy. Relle was right. He was grate-ful. He was grateful for the pasta and the bread with the fresh garlic from the garden. He was even grateful for the rain that kept them inside that afternoon. They all climbed the steps to the third floor of the mansion, where Gabe set up the radio equipment.

"What's this do?" Malachi asked. "What about this button?"

"I don't know," Gabe told him. The kids crowded around him. "Maybe someone else should do this. I'm not great with tech."

"I'm very good at it," Eric said, and Gabe had to force himself not to roll his eyes. "But you read the book."

"Right," Gabe said. He turned to the back cover, where Sam's name and call numbers were written. He would try that in a bit, when Sam got out of school. First, he wanted to see who else was out there. He told the others, and they inched closer. Outside, it thundered. Rain streamed down the windows. Barely visible, the water by the cliffs was wild and white.

"If we go through the frequencies, kind of like a radio in the car, we can hear from different places," he explained. "And everyone can hear us if we connect. It's public. So it's like a public phone conversation."

"Wait," Bear said. "How did a phone work? You could talk to lots of people or just one?"

Bear was too little to remember phone calls. Violet explained them to him while Gabe scanned. Everyone was quiet at the static sound. He turned up the volume and kept tuning higher. In the 135s, they heard: "We've got a patient coming in with what appears to be a fracture."

The kids squealed. Gabe's heart thrummed. A *patient?* That meant a clinic or a hospital. A *hospital.*

"Man, talk to them. Say something!" Malachi leaned on his shoulder. "What are you doing?"

"Okay," Gabe said. He held the button down and said his call number: N5MM2. "This is Gabe Sweeney in Maine. I live on an island with twenty-one other people. We just got a radio. This is our first . . ." He wrinkled his nose. "Contact? Call."

Silence answered.

"Well?" Eric said. "Where are they?"

"Sometimes you have to do it a few times." He hoped. He hoped it worked. Everyone was waiting. Gabe tried again. He repeated his call letters.

And a few seconds later: "Well, hello, Gabe. Welcome!" in a woman's voice.

"Heeyyyyy!" Malachi yelled. He squeezed Gabe's head. "You did it!"

Gabe grinned and bit his lip. "Hi," he spoke into the radio.

"This is Julia, the operator for Saint Mary's Hospital in Maryland."

They spent ten minutes talking to Julia. A real hospital! With doctors and nurses! For the next hour, they went through the frequencies and found people all over the country. An old couple in Seattle. Teenage girls in Florida. A college kid in Wyoming. And teachers and librarians in Buffalo.

Gabe was speechless. *All these people had survived.* When it was time to get ready for dinner, he turned it off. The kids stood in front of the windows and watched the storm at the edge of the world. Lightning cracked down over the ocean. A million possibilities echoed out there.

A few days later, on a Wednesday, Relle told him they were going to have a ceremony. Her face was very serious. She wore a black sleeveless sweater with a white, round collar under it. She did not look like herself. Wynnie and Violet stood behind her, their faces serious too. Gabe wondered if it was for the talent show. Or some skit.

"What kind of ceremony?" he asked. He was reading about antibiotics. Sylvia had told him he was allowed to make them as long as he kept the little kids away. The others were preparing for the talent show. It was going to

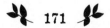

be Friday night, and all week the kids had been finishing up preparations, which were interfering with everything. Lessons, chores—that afternoon Sylvia had threatened to cancel it altogether if they didn't pay attention during their history lesson.

They had not paid attention.

But she had not canceled it.

Yet.

Whenever anyone asked Gabe about his talent, he mumbled something and changed the subject. It hadn't been easy.

"Is this about the talent show?" he asked Relle. She was so busy with preparations, he thought maybe she hadn't noticed he wasn't getting ready for it. *Did she know?* He closed the book.

"Don't worry about what the ceremony is, Sweeney! Let's go!" Wynnie said. They were wearing black too. And their hair had been braided and wound around their head.

Gabe looked at Relle and stood up. "Okay, Wynnie, let's have this ceremony!"

He followed Relle and Wynnie and Violet out of the library, out the big door, and down the front steps. "Where are we going?" he asked. They were all wearing black. He was not. "Are you going to kill me?" He was half serious. Their heads were bowed. They stopped and picked flowers along the edge of the garden, but no one answered him. "Should I get Malachi or Lucas?"

"I don't think so," Relle said. "I'm not sure they would appreciate it. I think this is more for the four of us."

"Sweeney," Wynnie said. "Chill."

Fine! He followed their lead and picked a handful of Queen Anne's lace. The stalks were tough to cut, and he had to use his thumbnail. Green juice lingered under his nail. He wiped it on his shorts.

They walked into the orchard. It smelled sweet and warm. Flies and bugs flew near his head. Relle stopped in front of a tree with glossy green leaves. Gabe hadn't noticed a rock in her hand, but she placed it at the base of the tree and then tipped her head and frowned. She adjusted it so it was flatter and stood.

Relle turned and faced her friends, her face very solemn. She closed her big eyes. "Dearly beloveds, we are gathered here today to celebrate . . ."

Gabe wondered if someone was getting married. It felt like that. But who?

"Royal Cornelius Balthasar—"

Roy. "Are you marrying your imaginary friend?"

"I swear to God, Sweeney," Wynnie said. "Sometimes you are so stupid."

"What?" he asked.

"Who we lay to rest this evening . . ." Relle clasped her hands together. "I first met Roy in June two summers ago, under the most glorious tree full of starlight."

Gabe didn't think that was scientifically accurate.

"He was from the South." She looked at her friends. "Obviously with a name like that. So romantic." She sighed. "He was a riverboat captain and the lead singer of a band that wore the most delightful, sensational outfits. They had a hit song that was all over the Internet." Relle shook her head and gazed into the blue sky. "All before he was fourteen."

Gabe bit his smile. He assumed that if you were day-dreamy enough to have an imaginary friend, you were daydreamy enough to have a funeral for them. He liked that she was weird. Relle made him think in different ways.

"But today, we say farewell to Roy." Relle clutched her heart. "My most faithful companion who helped me find this beautiful island with these wonderful people. I am forever grateful for your camaraderie. I will never forget your gallant ways. When you fought off a mountain lion.

When you saved that small kitten from a burning building. When you tenderly wrapped my injured ankle with a bandage."

Gabe had never felt jealous of a fictional person before, but he did now. Certainly those were all imagined victories, weren't they?

"Alas," Relle said. "It is time. I bid you goodbye and good luck, Roy. May you find peace on the other side."

Violet burst into tears when they threw their flowers on the rock. And when it was his turn, Gabe knelt down and placed the white flowers on the grave. He pressed his fingers to the rock. His heart fluttered a bit in worry. *It's not real,* he told himself. But it felt nice to be sad. He let it flood him.

"You were the handsomest man that ever lived," Violet wailed. Relle grasped her hand.

"We promise to take care of Relle while you're gone, Roy," Wynnie said.

The three of them looked at Gabe. Relle's eyes were big. He shifted on his feet. He cleared his throat. "I'm glad you were in the woods that day, Roy."

He wasn't even faking it to be nice to Relle.

When the ceremony was over, they walked back home through the thick green grass. Wynnie and Violet ran ahead, and Gabe took his time. "Are you sad?" he asked Relle.

He didn't look, but he felt her nod her head next to him.

"Yeah," he said. "I think that's okay and probably good."

And like she had done for him when Peter died, Gabe reached for her hand and folded it into his.

26

The day of the talent show, after dinner, the kids scattered to their rooms to get ready. Lucas tuned his guitar, his foot on his bed, his whole body leaning on the instrument and his knee. He was wearing nice pants and shiny shoes. A dress shirt that was striped and tucked into his pants. Gabe felt a little competitive with Lucas, which he knew was ridiculous. First, he wasn't even participating, and second, Lucas was going to do really well because he was good at singing and music. His sister would roll her eyes at him. *Not everything is a competition, Gabe.*

"You're going to do great, Lucas," Gabe said.

Downstairs, everyone was dressed either nicely, like it was a special occasion, or in a costume they'd found in one of the bedroom closets or the playroom. The little ones were pirates and fairies and knights. There was one mushroom, no asparagus.

A fairy skipped nearby. Gabe smiled. Everyone looked really happy. The whole house was buzzing.

Sylvia and Prerna gathered them all together, the small magical creatures, and led them out of the room through the big doors. They had set up all the chairs facing the fireplace at the front of the room, an aisle down their center. Relle was giving directions to Lucy and Mason.

Gabe's heart fluttered. She looked very pretty. Very Relle. She was wearing a white dress with enormous puffs of sleeves and flowers in her hair like a crown. It reminded him of when he'd found her. Gabe cleared his throat. Soon, like Peter had said, he was going to have to do something about this crush.

Gabe sat next to the aisle and watched Relle's red hair. She was bright and creative and brought beautiful things into people's lives. He loved that.

The youngest kids went first. It was a play Relle had written. The purple fairy, Alice, forgot her lines. And Bear said his line so loudly, the whole room laughed. A pirate carried Parth, who was dressed as a parrot. Gabe felt very warm and happy. Like his face couldn't frown if it tried. He clapped loudly when the little ones stood in a row, hand in hand, and bowed.

It was Relle's turn second. She twisted her hands together as she looked out at everyone, her face stark white, then launched into a story she had written. Some parts Gabe didn't get. But the others were, well . . . they were perfect. When she ran off stage, she floated down the aisle and a flower fell from her hair.

Gabe picked it up. It was next to him, after all.

And he tucked it in his shirt pocket and placed his hand against his chest while the others took their turns.

Wynnie juggled. Then Malachi, who flipped. And Violet, who sang with a sweet, clear voice along to Lucas on the piano. Chloe, Nora, and Prerna did a dance number. Wynnie's sister, Lucy, did stand-up comedy, and Gabe laughed even though the jokes were definitely not appropriate for a seven-year-old.

Mason was set to go next, but his guitar string broke, and the audience waited while Lucas replaced it. Baby Parth got restless and cried. Relle pressed her hands

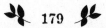

together, and she looked so worried about the mishap, Gabe's heart thumped. He hadn't prepared anything. He was the only one. And she cared so much. She had worked so hard.

Gabe's eyes burned. She had worked so hard because they still needed things to look forward to even though it was the end of the world. Gabe didn't want her to think the broken guitar string took anything away from all that hard work.

Gabe stood up. He needed to do something. He needed to fill that silence so that distraught look would leave her face. And what was wrong with him anyway? He thought he was too cool for a talent show or something? "I . . ." he said. Everyone looked at him. He wiped his palms on his pants. "Can I . . . ummm . . . can I go?"

"What are you gonna do, Sweeney?" Malachi yelled.

He had no idea. He walked to the front, where a little stage had been set up. Gabe turned and faced the audience. "I . . ." What could he do? He could whistle? No, he couldn't whistle. He shook his head and looked at Relle. She was watching him.

Gabe remembered how she had read to Peter. How her voice had soared, full of emotion. He could maybe do something like that. Read something. Only, he didn't have anything to read from, a book or a poem.

Songs were poems, weren't they? He couldn't sing, but maybe he could say a song like a poem. Gabe pressed his lips together. Yes, he could.

"I couldn't tell you before," he said. His voice shook. "But now it's all I can say." The cheesy first lines of the song by the singer Relle liked. Her favorite song.

"Aye!" Malachi yelled from his seat.

The kids giggled, but Gabe was serious. "Before you walk out that door . . . how do I make you stay?"

"Sweeeeeeeeeeney!"

Gabe finished the lyrics. He meant every word. He looked right at Relle Douglas because he didn't want to protect his heart anymore. And she looked right back.

When he was finished, he recited a poem. One for the kids. One his mother had read to him when he was little. It was silly and fun and made him happy to remember her.

Gabe went back to his seat to claps and felt energized and ready. His body was light. He felt like he could soar above the edge of the world.

***

When they finally went to sleep, which was much later than Sylvia wanted, Gabe felt like he was flying. He wasn't just happy. It was something else. It bubbled up within him. He was ecstatic. He unbuttoned his shirt and hung it back in the closet. Before, yes, he would have washed it, but to conserve water, they wore things twice. And that was good.

He pulled the flower out and put it on his nightstand. He whistled while he pulled the sheet back.

"Is that a flower?" Malachi asked. "Where'd you get that? Who did you get that from? Was it Relle? Uh-oh, Sweeney, you got it bad." Malachi enjoyed bothering him, but Gabe didn't care. Yes, he had it bad. It was wonderful.

Lucas was getting undressed. He had sung again after Mason as an unplanned encore and it was perfect, but Gabe barely heard it. His heart was thrumming with feeling.

"Lucas, you were really good," Gabe said.

"Too good," Malachi said. "Violet wanted nothing to do with me, and I blame you. For the rest of us, please keep your mouth closed. I can't be competing with the voice of an angel all the time. There's no winning! None!" He threw a pillow at their third roommate. "I'm about to fall in love with you myself!"

In the morning, Gabe ate his oatmeal, the happy streak continuing. He snuck glances at Relle. She was at the other end, laughing with Wynnie. Everyone was talking about the talent show. They agreed that Lucas had the best performance of the night, which didn't even bother Gabe's mood as he spooned raisins into his mouth. His sister was right; it was okay to let other people win. He was already winning. He grinned to himself for no reason.

A crush was fine.

A crush was better than fine. It was the best feeling in the world.

Gabe smiled his way through the next few weeks. Instead of groaning when they ate pasta, he enjoyed it. Pasta was good. Who cared if he needed to eat it every day? Sylvia made it flavorful and filling. Besides, sometimes he got to sit next to Relle and hold hands under the table.

One night at the end of July, Gabe went to the living room to set up the Scrabble board. They had played every night since the talent show. Sometimes other kids joined in, but his favorite was when it was just him and Relle. One glorious night, the whole island had watched them like it was a tennis match. Relle had won. Now Gabe put down the word *prize* and scored twenty points, but across from him, Relle had thirty.

Nora and Prerna came into the living room, the baby in Nora's arms. All three of them were beaming. "We have something to tell everyone!" Nora said.

Gabe glanced at his opponent. "Do you know what they're gonna say?" he whispered.

Relle nodded, her hands clasped under her chin.

"We're getting married," Prerna said. She grabbed Nora's hand. "In a few weeks, we decided. We'll have a big party and everything. We're happy, and finding happiness at the end of world is something we want to hold on to." The two looked at each other, and Gabe smiled. It made him feel hopeful and glad. He thought . . . well, he hadn't expected a real wedding again, and here one was.

The rest of the room felt the same. Relle leaped up, gushing words Gabe couldn't hear, she was speaking so fast. Malachi was whooping and cheering. And everyone crowded around them.

It was decided that everyone would go to the big island to get wedding supplies. Fancy clothes and wedding gowns. There was a dress shop from the Before. Prerna wanted a lehenga, but she wasn't sure the store would have the traditional Indian set.

Gabe congratulated them both, gave them a hug, then packed up the Scrabble box. He knew Relle wouldn't be back to finish the game. He shared her excitement about the wedding, but he didn't want to go back to the big island. He scowled and tapped his fingers on the table. He hadn't been back. Had avoided it at all costs. And now . . . Couldn't he just wear his khaki pants and button-down?

He didn't get a chance to think too much about it. The youngest kids came down from getting ready for bed. They heard the happy commotion of the wedding

announcement. Bear was wearing a striped pajama set. Blue and gray.

He stood in front of Gabe and rubbed his eye. "I don't feel good," he said.

Gabe's heart sank. It plummeted as far down as it could go. It crashed. "Oh, yeah?" He faked calm.

Bear crawled into Gabe's lap. He was warm. Too warm. Gabe put the back of his hand to Bear's head and then the back of his neck. Bear had a fever. Dread curled around Gabe's feet and snaked up his legs.

"Hey, buddy," he said to the little boy, "let's go upstairs and check your temperature." Gabe gently pulled the boy from his lap and stood him up.

"Okay," Bear said. Except he didn't move. He was flat and still and then vomited all over the carpet.

The whole room turned and stared at Bear and Gabe. Lucy said, "Gross, Bear."

"Lucy," Wynnie said. The rest of them were quiet. Vomiting reminded them of the end of the world.

"It's okay," Gabe said. "Probably just a little bug." He said it light. Hopefully reassuring. They had survived a bug in the winter that was similar. He squared his shoulders back like he believed himself. With one quick motion, he lifted the boy into a hug. "We're gonna go get cleaned up."

He held him close and left the room. Climbed the stairs with the too warm little body. Gabe put Bear down on the bathroom floor. He helped him with his pajamas. Got him into the tub and turned on the water. "I'll be right back," Gabe told him.

Gabe went to his room and changed. He put his dirty clothes and the messy pajamas into a laundry basket. When he went back to the bathroom, the tub was halfway full. He handed Bear a bucket in case he got sick again and found the thermometer.

It confirmed what Gabe suspected. Gabe washed his hands and leaned against the sink. He didn't want to freak out. A fever and vomiting could be a few things. Probably a bug. Most likely a bug. He wondered where it had come from.

"Do your ears hurt?" he asked.

Bear shook his head.

"How about your throat?" He would need antibiotics if it was an infection.

"No." Bear lay on his stomach in the water. "Do I have it?"

"Have what?" Gabe crossed his arms.

"The thing everyone's parents got."

"No," Gabe said. "No, you don't have that." But he couldn't be sure. Bear didn't have the rash across his cheeks, which was good. But Gabe didn't know if there was a new strain or . . . well. He bit his lip.

If it was a virus, it wasn't possible to contract it now. Gabe scowled. At least he didn't think it was possible. He and Wynnie had been home for a month. There was no way it had followed them. Clung to them. And wouldn't they all be sick, not just Bear?

"You'll be fine," Gabe said.

But still. It was a seed that rooted into the dirt. Gabe gave Bear Tylenol and new pajamas. Instead of putting him in his room with Ben and Tim, Gabe brought him to Peter's room to isolate. He didn't want the other kids to get sick, whatever it was.

They stood in the doorway, clean bedding in Gabe's arms.

"I don't want to sleep by myself," Bear whined. "It's scary."

Gabe understood. He couldn't remember the last time he'd slept in a room all by himself. "I'll sit in the chair."

Bear crawled into bed. "Promise? Promise you won't leave?"

"Promise. Honest."

Gabe sat in the chair as Bear slept. He felt frantic. He felt sole responsibility for the small body in the bed. *Did he have the virus? Was that even possible?* He'd have to check one of the books. *How long did viruses last?*

Gabe bounced his leg and worried every possible worry. When the older kids came up the stairs for bed, he worried more and more. *Would they get sick? Would they all get sick?* It was like Peter all over again. Gabe wasn't going to be able to stop anything from happening. He was powerless and somehow everyone else thought he could do something.

His throat burned. What could he do? He could hand out Tylenol. That was nothing.

He wished, so desperately, that his father were alive. That he were there, in the big house on the small island, and taking care of all of them. He needed his dad's reassuring words and steady hands.

Because Gabe couldn't do it.

He buried his face in his hands.

"Gabriel?" came from the hallway, and he shot up. Sylvia. He met her in the doorway.

"How is our youngest?" she asked.

"He has a fever and threw up," he told her. "But he's sleeping now."

"Hmm," she said. "Best not feed him too much tomorrow. He can have crackers. Maybe toast."

Gabe nodded. "I think if we watch it, it will pass soon. I'll just keep his fever down." Gabe knew fevers were the body fighting off an illness. They weren't bad necessarily. Just alarming. "I don't think it's an infection. Yet." He frowned.

Sylvia sighed. "I'm sorry you can't be fourteen."

Gabe didn't know what to say. Probably no one at the end of the world got to act their age.

"Go get some sleep, Gabe," Sylvia patted him on the shoulder. "I can stay with him."

Gabe didn't want to argue with Sylvia, but he couldn't leave Bear. "I won't be able to sleep anyway. And you already do everything for all of us. I can stay."

So Gabe spent a sleepless night with the sick boy.

When the first bit of light peeked in the windows, Gabe woke with a start. He shot up from the chair and looked over at little Bear, asleep in the bed. *He was so stupid! So stupid! He had to be the stupidest human alive!* Gabe sprinted up the stairs. Skipped steps. Ran down the hall and stared at the ham radio.

They weren't alone anymore. And he didn't need to pout in the dark. He was annoyed with himself as he called out to the hospital in Maryland. They answered right away, a different operator than last time.

"Hi, this is Gabe Sweeney, and I was hoping I could talk to a nurse or a doctor."

"I'll be right back," the operator said.

Gabe closed his eyes in relief, and when the doctor spoke, Gabe explained what was wrong with Bear. "He can't keep anything down."

"Start with the BRAT diet. I'm not sure of your resources, but bananas, rice, applesauce, and toast. Would you have access to any of those?"

"Yeah," Gabe said. "No bananas, but the rest."

"And probiotics. He can take those."

Gabe thought he had those. "Do you think it's whatever made the world end?"

"Hmm," the doctor said, "I do not. It is possible, but I would assume it is a separate virus. If he didn't get it the first time, he probably won't have it now."

"You're sure?" Gabe's voice shook.

"As sure as I can be," she said. Her Southern accent was soft. "Has anyone been traveling in the last month? Or anyone new to the community?"

Gabe nodded as he spoke, "Yes, both."

"I would continue to monitor his symptoms. It sounds like he's been exposed to something in your travels, and since he's young, his body may not have seen the illness before. It will most likely pass. If you want to check back

in, though, you may. We have doctors to answer questions for anyone on the radio. That's why we have the operator. It's an old-fashioned WebMD." She laughed.

"Thank you." Gabe put his face in his hands and sighed. He let his shoulders fall. The relief he felt. That his assessment was right, that the doctor was so easy to contact, that he could call her again if he didn't know the dosage or the right medication.

Gabe walked downstairs and checked Bear's temperature again. It was still high. He gave him Tylenol and sat and waited with his small patient. The other kids were leaving for the big island, and he was grateful not to go with them. Having doctor duties was a good excuse.

Relle appeared in the doorway, and Gabe joined her.

"You're not going to the island?" Relle asked. "I've never been. I do want some pretty clothes. I can't decide if I want something terribly romantic or divinely chic for the wedding." She clasped her hands together.

"Why not both?" He smiled. "No, I'm going to stay with Bear." He turned and looked at the little boy, who was coloring in bed.

"Bear, would you like anything special from the big island?" Relle asked.

"A toy," he said. "A dinosaur! The biggest one you can find!"

"I can do that," Relle said. She looked very deep into Gabe's eyes, and Gabe both loved that and wished that she wouldn't. "You don't go to the big island, do you?"

"Ah," he said. He knew, if it had been someone else, he would have faked his words, but he didn't feel like he had to do that with Relle. "No."

"I can imagine it would be very painful to return. I, for one, am not sure I could ever return to my house. But I suppose there could come a time in my life where I *might* want to. To soothe my soul perhaps."

Gabe's soul was very tired. "That's a good idea." Though which part, he wasn't sure.

Someone downstairs yelled up for her.

"Wynnie wants to get you a blue tuxedo," she said. "With ruffles. They want to match you."

He smiled again. "Wynnie is allowed to pick out whatever they want me to wear, and I will wear it with pride."

"Okay," she said. "Bye!" Relle touched him on the arm. Gabe liked that a lot. He didn't want her to leave.

When she did, he turned around to face Bear. "Looks like it's just you and me. What do you want to do?"

"Play dinosaurs!"

"Okay, let's play dinosaurs."

Gabe played dinosaurs. And monitored Bear. For three days, Sylvia made small servings of toast and rice, and Gabe fed Bear. It worked. On the fourth day, it was like Bear had never been sick at all. He hopped off the bed and ate a piece of thick bread with blueberry jam and goat cheese.

Gabe could finally breathe again. But it had taken its toll. He hadn't slept much, and when he did, it was fretful and unsettled. Just like his waking moments.

Gabe knew that Relle was right. That his soul had not really healed from his family or from Peter. And when Bear got sick, well . . . everything unhealed broke back open.

Gabe needed to do some healing.

On a Wednesday morning in August, after breakfast, Gabe pulled Relle aside. He didn't have chores until the evening, and he needed to go back to the big island. To his home. Or his old home. He wasn't sure what to call it anymore.

"I'm gonna skip lessons this morning. I already told Sylvia," he said. He held both of Relle's hands in his. "I have to go home. You were right about the soul . . . healing part, I think." He cleared his throat.

"Do you want me to go with you?" she asked.

Gabe shook his head. He did, but he didn't. He wasn't sure what the island would do to him. "Can we play Scrabble when I get back?" *Or a walk to the orchard or the rocks,* he thought. Really anything.

"I'm not sure why you like losing so badly, but yes."

Gabe laughed. "It's a date." He didn't know if people went on dates in the new version of the world or if Scrabble counted as a date, but he wanted to test the word aloud.

"Gabe," Relle said, her chin out, "do you want to go to the wedding together? As a date?"

"Yeah," he said. "Yeah, I do want to do that."

Relle smiled very big. And then hugged him fiercely. "Good luck today. It is a very brave thing you are doing."

He wasn't sure he was brave enough for it yet.

Gabe walked down to the rowboat with Mud by his side. It was not spring like when he'd found Relle, but a warm summer full of green. The sun was hot. He rolled up his pants and let the water run over his feet. He whistled, not out of hope and anticipation, but for Mud to hop in the boat, which she did.

Gabe checked the boat like usual, then pushed off against the rocks. He felt sick to his stomach. From lack of sleep. From nerves. Gabe sighed loudly. He did not want to go home. Not at all. But he rowed toward the island.

By the time he got to the other shore, he was sweating. He pushed up his short sleeves so that they bunched around his shoulders. He needed to give himself a pep talk. He didn't want to. He didn't want to climb the shore to the road that made a horseshoe around the island. He wanted to step back in the boat and speed across the water and sit in the library, reading about how the lungs worked or something.

"No, you don't," he said aloud. He sounded like Relle. Like he was very close to being someone who talked to imaginary friends, but even she was done with that now. Gabe turned his attention to Mud, because talking to a dog at least made sense. "We are going to go to the house, and we are going to say goodbye properly."

Because he never had.

Gabe climbed the hill. A deer ate from overgrown blueberry bushes. Mud pointed at it, and Gabe whistled her away. "Don't chase deer, Muddy."

At the top of the hill was a path. It was overgrown like the bushes, and Gabe stepped carefully, pushing down grasses with his arms and shoes. He could barely see Mud's back through the green. A snake shot away from the boy, and Gabe was equally startled.

The path turned into a road, and this, Gabe followed. It headed into town on the north end of the island. He passed classmates' houses and soccer fields. The library. The clinic where his father worked. There, Gabe paused, shaking. He leaned his hands against his knees and got sick. When he was done, he wiped his mouth with the back of his hand.

It was a terrible idea, he decided. A terrible idea to come back here. *How could the others do this?* See this place again. It was revisiting a nightmare.

Gabe turned around. That was enough. He'd tried. He'd go back to the small island, he'd go home. He wouldn't let himself get anxious when the others got sick with fevers. That was all he had to do. Not get anxious.

He rolled his head back. That wasn't how it worked. Gabe groaned up at the blue sky. *Why wasn't any of this easy? Why?! It wasn't fair. None of it was fair!* He wanted to worry about stupid stuff like if he passed his English test or if he forgot his math homework or if his lacrosse cleats were in the laundry room instead of his backpack!

Gabe yelled.

He yelled louder and louder.

He did not want to worry about being in charge of other people's lives when they got sick. He couldn't do it. He wasn't his father. Someone else could do it! Why did it have to be his responsibility?!

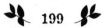

Gabe yelled again. Into the woods. Into the green Maine island. Into the overgrown old world.

Until his voice was raw. Until snot and tears dripped down his face.

And then he took a deep breath.

It didn't matter why it was his responsibility. It was. And he could either accept that or throw tantrums every time someone got sick or hurt.

"Yeah, Sweeney," he said aloud.

Gabe followed Main Street, past the shops the others had been to earlier, the doors nicely shut for the next time they needed clothes. He turned down Sea Lane and stood in front of the house at the end. It was tall and white with white shutters and a gray door. The winter had been hard on the paint. Gabe pursed his mouth like he was going to whistle and blew air in a steady way to comfort himself.

At the top of the steps, Gabe rested his hand on his dog's head. She was excited and wiggled. The door was not locked. He turned the knob, and Mud nosed her way into the house first.

More than anything, Gabe did not want to go into the house. He crossed his arms. Then uncrossed them. Then mumbled to himself.

"Okay!" he said.

And he stepped through the doorway.

It smelled like his house. It smelled like his mom and dad and sister and their laundry detergent and whatever it was that made a family smell like one another. A lump formed in his throat that only eased a bit when he cried out.

The living room was a little messy. A blanket on the floor. Tissues crumpled on the wood coffee table. His lacrosse bag next to the door. He picked up his stick. Punched the laces. He and his dad had gone to Portland to get it for his twelfth birthday. Gabe put it down gently. He stepped over to the blanket and folded it, draping it on the couch. Gathered the tissues and took them into the kitchen.

He threw them out in the garbage. It smelled like onions, and he opened the pantry to find onions growing out of a bag. That made him smile. There was still life inside a dark pantry, shut off from the world.

Gabe walked up the stairs to his room. It was full of things he used to think were important. Papers from school. His yearbook from sixth grade. Trophies from lacrosse and basketball. Everything was dusty. He sat down on the floor and flipped through the yearbook. He smiled at some things he remembered. Field trips. Spirit Weeks. The drama club production of *A Christmas Carol*. And felt a sadness in his chest at others. At girls he had liked. At boys he had played sports with.

He said goodbye to his room and shut the door. Across the hall was his sister's room. Caroline. She had been ten. Her room was the color of sea glass. She'd liked mermaids, and their mom had decorated her room with sea art and shell garland. It smelled so much like Caroline, like something sweet, a fruit maybe, Gabe gasped. He sat on her bed.

"Hey," he said. "I just . . ." he cried. "I miss you." Gabe bit on his wrist, and tears ran down his face. "I really miss you, Care. I just . . . you would have had Ms. Shaw this year maybe. She was great." He didn't know

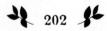

why he said that, but it felt nice to talk to her. Caroline would have thought Ms. Shaw was funny. "I'm trying." Trying to be less competitive. Trying to grow and do his best. It would have been easier with her around.

When he stopped crying, Gabe straightened her sheets and blankets and opened the curtains to let the sun in. He slipped a pair of her swim goggles into his pocket. She had been a great swimmer. He patted the doorway when he left.

In his parents' room, he stepped into his mother's closet and touched her shoes. It smelled like her perfume, the clothes did, and he stood there with his eyes closed, surrounded by her. His mother had been very peaceful and gentle and practical. She grew fat tomatoes in the backyard. He took a ring out of her jewelry box, one that had belonged to his grandmother. It was a round pearl with tiny diamonds around it, and he let it join the goggles.

"Love you, Mom," he whispered. "Thank you for watching apocalypse movies with me."

Gabe most associated the office with his dad, so he went downstairs to say goodbye to him there. Gabe sat very still at his father's desk, not moving for a long time, maybe minutes, maybe hours. And his face was completely dry. A calm settled over the boy.

To the reflection in the blank computer screen, Gabe finally spoke. He told him about Peter. And Bear getting sick. And what medical textbooks he'd been reading. And how he had called on the ham radio. His dad would have liked the technology. He told him about Relle and the wedding. And Relle again.

"You would like her, Dad. She's really smart." He laughed. "Much smarter than I am. I have to work really hard to keep up with her." Gabe smiled. "Really, if anyone should be a doctor, it's her."

He stood up and went over to the rows of books. He pulled out one called *When There Is No Doctor* and hugged it to his chest.

"I'll be back," he said. "Honest. I'll come all the time."

And he meant it. His soul felt clear. And he vowed to come back whenever it didn't.

31

Gabe hugged his dog and patted her head. He nuz-
zled his face against her. "Okay," he said. "Let's go home."

The two of them walked through town. Gabe stopped
in the wedding dress shop. The suit Wynnie had brought
back was too small, so he needed something else. When
he didn't find suits, he went to the store next to it and
found all the suits he could ever need. He tried on a pale
pair of pants and a short-sleeve shirt that was white and
crisp. And tan loafers. It was all much better than what
he had worn to the talent show.

He looked himself over in the mirror and was pretty proud. He put his shoulders back and felt a little more like Gabe Sweeney than he had lately. "I look pretty good, don't I, Muddy?" He turned and looked at his back. "I do!"

Gabe wondered if maybe Relle would kiss him. Because of the outfit or because she was happy for the wedding or just because she liked him and wanted to kiss him too. Yes, he decided, she probably did.

A lightness filled him—one he hadn't felt in a long time. The world felt very full of possibility and wonder. He smiled as he walked, with his bag of clothes and the things from his old house, down the road and path to the boat.

He put everything on a pad in the front so it wouldn't get wet and tied the bag up tight. Mud jumped in and stood, her front feet on the bench. Gabe stood in the boat before he pushed off, the water lapping the sides, with his hands on his hips. A grin on his face.

His soul felt . . . well . . . not perfectly healed, but settled. Content. It stayed with him across the water, on the beach, down the Avenue. He patted one of the goats in the great green yard and stared up at the big house.

He had things to do.

It was almost two o'clock. Everyone would be finishing their afternoon reading time, and then they would

be free until dinner. Gabe needed to clean himself up, brush his teeth. He ran upstairs and did that and changed his shirt.

He passed Malachi on the way back down the stairs. "Hey, gonna play lacrosse, you want to?"

"Yeah, in a little bit," Gabe said. There was a red-haired girl he had to talk to. And possibly kiss.

He found her in the garden, with Violet and Wynnie. They were looking for four-leaf clovers in a patch that always produced them. Like magic.

"It's like tiny men with gold in their pockets spilled out a bit of luck right here in our grass," Relle said, her face down.

"Hey," he said. He worried his boldness would slip away. Disappear like morning fog. But it was right there.

Relle sat up. She peered at him and blinked in the sunshine. Oh boy, he was so in love with her, it was stupid. "How is your soul, Gabe?"

"It's good. It's really good. Hey, come with me." Anywhere. Really anywhere. "Please. If you want to." Like tacking on those words made it feel less urgent.

"Farewell, dear ones," she said to the others. She stood and twirled a piece of Violet's hair. "If you find a wicked sprite, please come find me so that I too can delight in his mischief."

Relle turned to him. "Where should we go?"

He didn't care.

"Let's go to the little bridge over the stream," she said. "It's where I do my best daydreaming." She scowled. "Though I did drop my notebook in there once when I got particularly distracted. And even though I fished it out, it was ruined. I'll try not to hold the stream personally accountable."

Gabe walked silently to the bridge, which was fine because Relle talked the whole way. He was not sure how it was supposed to go. How did you declare your love? Did you? Didn't he already tell her in the note? And was he supposed to say it like a speech or . . . well, he wasn't quite sure what he was doing.

They stood on the bridge. It was small, only a few feet across, and most definitely unnecessary, but Gabe figured the rich owners of the house wanted a bridge, so they got a bridge.

"Relle," he said, which seemed like a good starting point. "I just . . . well, I've been thinking."

"I have too," Relle said. Her face was very solemn, and Gabe panicked.

"You have?" His gut fell. Just like her notebook, it tumbled into the water. He cleared his throat. Okay, well, if she was going to tell him she didn't like him or something, he could handle it. *Couldn't he?* He braced himself.

"Yes, I didn't know Peter as well as you did, and I should have been more sensitive to you asking me to postpone the talent show. Sometimes I have a tendency to rush, and I rushed that."

"Oh," he said. *Was that all?* His gut yanked itself out of the water. "That's . . . thank you. The talent show was really nice. You did a good job organizing it. I should have been more supportive of it."

"What were you thinking? I interrupted you." She tipped her chin at him, and her eyes were wide.

"I like you," Gabe said. "I just really like you and wanted to tell you that because I know I said it in the letter, but I really do."

Relle laughed. "I really like you too."

Gabe liked her laugh a lot. It was warm and big. "And you were right, going back to the island was . . . well, it was really good for me. I was worried I just couldn't do this fake doctor thing, and now I feel better."

"You won't be a fake anything, Gabe Sweeney," she said. "Everything you do is in earnest."

Yes, she definitely had power over him when she said his name. He was sure of it. What he wasn't sure of was how to bring up kissing. *Did you just say it? Did you ask?* No one told him. And Violet had just kissed him. He hadn't known it was coming.

"Relle, I was . . . Do you . . . Can we . . ."

Sweeney! Get it together! What is wrong with you? Where is the confidence of the suit shop?! GO!

"Can I kiss you?" he blurted.

"Yes."

That made his heart pound very, very hard. He moved closer to her. Very, very close. Her mouth was a breath away. But even a breath away was too far. So he fixed that.

He leaned into her and pressed his lips to hers. They were soft and kissed his back. He broke away for a second and watched her mouth. *Was it real? Had they really kissed? Or had he imagined it like he'd been thinking about for weeks?*

Relle placed her hand on his arm.

And pinched him. Hard.

"Did you pinch me?!"

"I had to make sure it was real," she said.

Gabe smiled. It was definitely real. And he wanted to do it more. He held on to her arm, above her elbow, and kissed her again.

32

In August, just like with the talent show, the wedding consumed the island. Preparations were made. Flowers were argued about. Chairs and tables rearranged and organized. But Gabe spent the days before it wandering around in a haze. A grinning, goofy haze. All of it was beautiful. He had no opinion except for that.

Gabe was in charge of cleaning up the front yard for the ceremony. He had to rake up goat poop, which was maybe the worst chore to have, but he didn't mind. Whistling helped. Actually, he was totally fine with it. He had someone he liked kissing and a plan for the next few months. Everything felt right. His soul . . . well, it felt wonderful.

He leaned against the rake, and Prerna came up to him, waving and chatting about the lawn and how good it looked. She wore a bright red dress, and her hair was curly and down. Gabe couldn't believe that not very long ago she was pointing a gun at him. It made him smile.

"Gabe, I have a question for you about the wedding."

"Yeah?" He straightened up and tried to focus.

"So tomorrow would be the ceremony where the couple's families meet and ask Ganesh for blessings and fortune. And Nora has her family, of course, but I was hoping with Parth, you and Wynnie could represent my family since you both brought me here."

"Yeah," Gabe said. Sometimes family was found. With a gun pointed at you. "I'd love to! Thank you." He hugged Prerna. She was twenty-two and the closest thing he'd ever had to an older sister. Of course he would be her family. And Caroline would have loved her. He was proud to have two sisters.

The next evening, he and Wynnie sat together on the couch, Parth squirming between them as the brides joined the two families together. Gabe felt very warm and happy acting as someone's family. He felt a peacefulness that he hadn't expected to ever feel again. Parth kissed him on the cheek and it was wet.

The night before the vows was the sangeet, which started with a big meal that Sylvia made with five of the others. Gabe had not been part of that; he had helped build the stage that they would take in a few minutes. Eric had organized the stage building. He wasn't as patient as Peter, but the work looked neat and professional. Peter would have been proud.

The table was loud and energetic as they ate daal, lentils with cumin and garlic. Relle sat next to Gabe, and he turned and smiled at her. He was very lucky and wholly grateful.

When the dishes had been cleared away, it was time for the dances and performances. Prerna taught them a few as a group, and it was funny and happy to mess up and watch others laugh and trip over one another. They all agreed that Violet had done the best job.

Gabe went to sleep like it was Christmas night. Full and content.

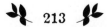

In the morning, he walked all over the island before the others were awake. He stopped at the edge of the world and watched the rocks below. It was as calm as the edge of the world got. Gabe felt calm and peaceful too.

Mud trotted behind as Gabe followed the curve of the island to the beach. He threw a stick in the water, and his dog ran after it. In the southern corner, he picked blueberries, then made his way back through the orchard. He told Roy good morning as he passed his rock.

Gabe walked toward the big yard, and Relle was standing on the stage, her hands on her hips. She climbed a ladder and attached flowers to the canopy. They were pink and white and blue. Great full things. He didn't know where she'd gotten them. Maybe down by the orchard. In the field where they had picked Queen Anne's lace. He stood at the bottom of the ladder and held it steady for her.

"Hey," he said.

"Gabe," she said. "How does it look? I can't tell from up here."

"Perfect." It was true. They stood under a dream.

She beamed. "I have to add more," she said. "Are you

excited for the wedding? I'm excited. It'll be desperately romantic, I think. We've been working so hard. And Nora and Prerna are both so lovely, even though I would still be excited even if they were ugly. Don't tell anyone I said that. And isn't it nice to know there's love even when the world is rebuilding?"

Gabe nodded. It was nice. But he already knew that there was love even when the world was rebuilding. He'd known it for a while now.

Relle came back down and gathered a bunch of greens. "Can you hand me these when I get up there?" she asked. She pushed them into his chest and climbed the ladder again.

Gabe helped her, and then he cleaned up more goat poop. In the gardens, he and Malachi checked on the squash and pumpkins they had planted a few days before. They were using the schedule Peter had taught them. The two of them plucked tomatoes from their vines and brought them into the kitchen.

When it was time to get ready for the wedding, he washed his hands and face and changed into the clothes from his trip to the suit shop in his bedroom.

"Oooooooh," Malachi yelled. "Looking good, Sweeney! Not as good as me, but . . . " Malachi ran his hand over his collar.

"No one ever can," Gabe said. He slid on his shoes.

"Who you gonna dance with tonight, Lucas?" Malachi asked. He danced in the mirror and watched himself.

"Maybe Violet," Lucas said. "She kissed me after the talent show."

Gabe grinned. He was happy for them.

"Okay," Malachi said. He shook Lucas's shoulders happily. "Okay! Ready?"

Downstairs was chaotic. Prerna was getting ready in the office, and Nora in the library, and girls ran between the two rooms across the great big hall.

"Go sit down!" someone yelled. "We're starting!" And the kids rushed out the front door.

Gabe sat and Relle joined him. She was wearing a huge ball gown that would look ridiculous at a wedding Before, but today looked right. It was pale blue and sheer with long sleeves and flowers all over it, both printed and sewn on. And in her hair were small flowers. Gabe leaned close to her. "You look really pretty."

She smiled. "And you look exceedingly handsome, Gabe."

They both smiled a lot. And the ceremony started, but to Gabe, it was hard to keep his eyes on the two celebrating. He snuck glances at Relle, her hand in his hand. It felt almost obscene how happy he was.

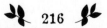

Under the flowers that Relle had arranged, Nora and Prerna, in their white and red, exchanged garlands of flowers and circled around a small fire that Eric watched with a careful eye. They vowed and promised. And there was powder on foreheads and black beaded necklaces and rings.

The people of the island ate dinner and a strawberry cake and Sylvia let Lucas hook up speakers that blasted in the August evening. They danced to songs that were older than Gabe and songs that had been popular three years ago and songs that reminded Gabe of his family. It was perfect.

He danced real slow with Relle, and it was the best thing maybe ever. He could have done that forever. Gabe figured the end of eighth grade dance had nothing on Nora and Prerna's wedding.

When the sky turned purple, and the music switched to a fast song, Gabe asked Relle, "Can we go to the edge of the world?"

"I was going to ask the same thing." Relle took his hand, and they left the party. They passed Lucas and Violet, and Gabe waved to his friends. He and Relle headed for the rocks, her dress a cloud around her.

"This is my favorite spot," Relle said. "I think I dreamed about this place before I even knew it existed. And now it not only exists, but it belongs to me."

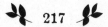

He needed to talk to her about him leaving this spot. But he didn't want to.

Instead, he kissed her. Or she kissed him, he wasn't sure. It didn't really matter. When they stopped for a moment, he said, "Relle. You know I'm doing that workbook." Since he'd talked to the doctor on the radio, he had been working through a medical textbook she'd recommended with questions in the back.

She nodded and fanned out the skirt of her dress. Her hair had gotten wild. Gabe liked it. It reminded him of when they first met.

"I should be done with it in the spring," he told her.

"Gabe. It feels like you have something to say, so say it. I can handle it." Relle stuck her chin out. It was very defiant. And he liked that most of all.

"When I'm done, I'd like to go to Maryland. I've been talking to one of the doctors there. She agreed to let me study under her."

"Like a mentorship?" she asked.

"Yeah."

"Gabe!" She grabbed his hand. "I think that's a wonderful idea!"

"You do?"

"Yes! Why wouldn't I?" She flounced out her skirt again. She looked like she enjoyed doing it. "I think it sounds like an adventure. I was a little envious when you went to the base. I was pretty sick of traveling at that point, but it is nice to go see the rest of the world. And it's hard to teach yourself years of medical schooling." Her eyes went wide. Her finger went up. "I have an idea."

"What is it?" Gabe sat in the grass.

Relle joined him, and her dress floated around her as she sat. "I'm going to learn the workbook with you," she said. "That way, when you're gone, we'll have a substitute doctor. And also, I'm pretty sure I'll not only keep up with you, but I'll probably do better on the quizzes."

Gabe grinned. "Oh, you will?"

"Yes, as we've seen from Scrabble, I'm much smarter than you are."

The boy could not stop smiling, no matter how hard he tried. He pulled a flower out of her red flame of hair. "I don't think that's possible. I'm going to win. You have no chance. I've been training for months already." He fake flexed. "I will destroy you, Relle. Like when I won that one Scrabble game, do you remember that? I think it was like one hundred points or something. One hundred and seven maybe?"

She narrowed her eyes at him. "I don't recall that. We will have to make a wager."

"Whatever you want. What do you want, Relle?"

"I want to beat you on that test."

Gabe laughed.

"No," she said. "I think it is important to have goals. I think I'd like to be a teacher. I'd like to help Sylvia and Nora with that. My parents were both teachers. That's how they met. They worked at the same high school. He taught biology and she taught English." She smiled. "So, Gabe Sweeney, I will help you study to be a doctor and you will help me study to be a teacher."

"That sounds like a good plan." Gabe wanted nothing more, well . . . maybe that was not true. But for now, this was perfect. It wasn't possible to be happier. He wrapped Relle's hand in his and they stared at the edge of the world, her head on his shoulder.

Author's Note

The first time I encountered Anne Shirley, I was seven or eight, and my dad said, "I think you might like this." To say that I liked the PBS miniseries *Anne of Green Gables* would be an understatement. I saw myself in Anne's temper. In her love of beautiful things and flowery words. In her competitive spirit. And I was thoroughly in love with Jonathan Crombie's Gilbert Blythe.

Through elementary and middle school, I watched and rewatched the rented tape from the public library and read the entire series. I moved to L. M. Montgomery's other works, but it was Anne and Gilbert whom I loved the most. I loved them when they were students in Avonlea. I loved them when they were academic rivals in college. I loved them when they were parents.

I shifted to different writers and influences when I was older, but little nods to Anne and Gil still cropped up in my writing. Mary Murphy, from my debut *Mary Underwater*, wears signature braids, and her love interest, Kip Dwyer, winks at her a lot like Gil winks at Anne.

In 2019, I finished editing *Mary* and didn't know what to work on next. I started a few middle-grade projects that fell flat. I panicked that I wouldn't ever write another book. In December, the third season of *Anne with an E* premiered on Netflix. I watched it over Christmas break and felt the same affection for the characters of my youth.

My agent had once asked me to write an Anne Shirley-meets–*Terminator* book, which I thought was absolutely ridiculous, but to pull me out of my writing drought, I wondered if writing with already established characters might make it easier to finish another book. Even if I didn't show anyone. Even if it didn't sell.

I brainstormed ways to make *Anne of Green Gables* current. But wasn't it already current? Putting Anne opposite Gil as two competing student body presidents didn't feel revolutionary like the original. I wanted not the present and not the past. So the future. And part of the magic of Avonlea to me was the lush, green island setting. So I wanted green. A gentle, green end of the world.

I set to work researching the end of the world. I read prepper books. To achieve a green apocalypse, I decided to create a pandemic like the flu in 1918–1919. At the end of 2019, I started writing *Gabe in the After*. My kids and I watched zombie and apocalypse movies. News of the novel coronavirus popped up in my googling. I texted my friends while I researched. "Have you heard about this?" and "This virus doesn't sound good." But I never imagined its magnitude.

In March 2020, I finished my book and sent it to my agent, and the United States started our lockdown. In Texas, my kids and I planted a bean garden and made soft pretzels. We only left the house to walk our dogs down the street. My agent made negotiations while my book tour for *Mary Underwater* was canceled because of the virus.

By the time *Gabe in the After* went to edits, the United States had been experiencing COVID-19 for over a year. It changed details in this book. It also changed the world. Many of us have suffered great tragedies in that time. We've missed important milestones and altered the way we live. We've lost family members and friends.

But, like Gabe, we've also experienced new beginnings. We've celebrated birthdays and had first crushes. We've welcomed babies into our families and learned how to connect in new ways.

New experiences don't take away from our losses, but they give us hope. My wish for you, reader, is to experience hope—that beautiful, powerful thing—amid all the tragedy.

Acknowledgments

For my children, June, Teddy, and Dwyer, thank you for, like Gabe and his mom, watching postapocalyptic movies with me and endlessly discussing how to survive the end of the world while we navigated 2020. I would blow up a million zombies for you.

To my agent, Veronica Park, who in 2016, told me to write an Anne Shirley-meets-*Terminator* middle-grade novel, and groaned in 2020 when I told her it was Gilbert Blythe meets *The Road*, thank you for letting me write strange things.

To my editor, Erica Finkel, thank you for loving both romance and adventure and for your always immaculate eye for story. Your brilliance and attention to detail amaze me.

To the rest of the team at Abrams and Amulet, especially Emily Daluga, Jenn Jimenez, Amy Vreeland, Jade Rector, Andrew Smith, Minnie Phan, Regina Castillo, Jenny Choy, Trish McNamara O'Neill, and Rey Noble, thank you for all your hard and thoughtful work.

Thank you to my early readers. The McKinnon family for naming Mud. Lucas Hauger and Jacob Seitz.

Ms. Pearlman's eighth-grade English class, I was terrified to share with you, but you were an immense help with my opening chapters. Lorien Lawrence, this story and the planet are better because of you. Prerna Pickett, thank you for your encouraging words while I was drafting and editing and launching. I'm sure you would survive the end of the world like your namesake. Amanda Fazzio, you are a blessing of a critique partner.

To my other publishing besties, Samantha Cohoe, Jeff Bishop, Jenny Elder Moke, Janae Marks, and Tanya Guerrero, I would not have made it through 2020 without you. You're the best.

Toj, thank you for running on my side of the road.

And finally, thank you to my parents for introducing me to Anne Shirley and Gilbert Blythe and Avonlea. I will forever be grateful for knowing this story and its beautiful green world. Thank you for showing me that God is in nature and nature is in God.

About the Author

Shannon Doleski is the author of *Mary Underwater*. After graduating from Niagara University with an English Education degree, she was a high school and middle school teacher and swim coach in New York and Maryland. She lives in a very loud house with her three children, a speckle-eared beagle, and an ornery dachshund. To learn more about Shannon, visit shannondoleski.com.